Exciting adventure on an alien world is yours as YOU find yourself stranded on the forbidding planet Volturnus. You control your fate as you battle the evil space pirates, strange and shapeless Dralasites, or the terrible quickdeath monster!

What will you do?

Having sought help from a spiderlike alien tribe, you must undergo the Ritual of the Quickdeath before they will believe you intend them no harm and will give you aid.

1) "Don't do it, Kyiki!" says your Compu-Pal friend, Ting. "I can't see the creature, but it sounds terrible. Don't take chances!" If this is your choice, turn to page 35.

2) "But surely I should do whatever I can to get home, including fighting this horrible creature," you reply. If this is your choice, turn to page 124.

Whichever path you pick, you are sure to find adventure, as you encounter the

VILLAINS OF VOLTURNUS

-ROSLOF

An ENDLESS QUEST™ Book #8

VILLAINS of VOLTURNUS

BY JEAN BLASHFIELD

Cover Art by Elmore
Interior Art by Jim Roslof

TSR Hobbies, Inc.

For Winnie — more delightful than fiction.

Distributed to the book trade in the United States by Random House, Inc. and in Canada by Random House of Canada, Ltd.
Distributed in the United Kingdom by TSR (UK), Ltd.
Distributed to the toy and hobby trade by regional distributors.

First Printing: May, 1983
Printed in the United States of America
Library of Congress Catalog Card Number: 82-51208
ISBN: 0-88038-023-3

9 8 7 6 5 4 3 2 1

TSR Hobbies, Inc.
P.O.Box 756
Lake Geneva, WI 53147

TSR Hobbies (UK), Ltd.
The Mill, Rathmore Road
Cambridge CB1 4AD
United Kingdom

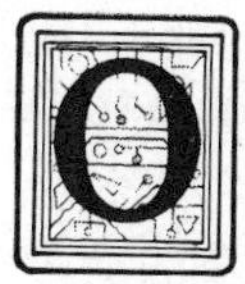ur orbit is not holding! Our ship is falling into the atmosphere toward Volturnus!"

You hear a gulp, then the captain's voice comes over the speaker again. "Please proceed to the rescue capsule. Remain calm, and remember emergency procedures."

"Wow!" you exclaim. "That's one way to see a new planet!" You turn excitedly toward Jac, your tutor, but the unflappable eight-legged Vrusk is not in the special seat designed to hold his long body.

When you left your home planet yesterday, you expected just another ho-hum field trip. You've been seeing pictures of Volturnus for months now. After all, your father's company, Universal Minerals, is exploring it for mineral resources. In fact, the spaceship you are on is a research craft from Universal Minerals.

"Where should I go?" you ask a scientist hurrying past, pulling his weightless body along with the aid of built-in handholds.

"Get to the capsule," he snaps. "I've got to pack my records. Sorry, kid." And he pulls himself hurriedly into the laboratory.

You pause to see if you should pack anything. All you have is what is in your pouches: argonstick, Uni-pen, vibroknife, Stunstick, microreader, firecell, electronic chess set. Ting, your Compu-Pal, sits in his case on the seat back above you. You touch the personal radio crystal on its chain around your neck. With

Ting to talk to and play electronic chess with, you're all set if you have to wait awhile to be picked up.

"Get a move on, Kyiki!" urges a passing technician, laden with mineral samples.

There's still no sign of Jac, so you decide to go directly to a rescue pod. You grab Ting and release your safety belt.

You float from your seat to a corner. On your left is a hatch labeled "Personal Safety Pod." PSPs are tiny landing vehicles that hold only one or two people. They are dropped from a spaceship to the surface of a planet while the main ship stays in orbit. Later, a shuttle comes to pick them up.

On your right, the corridor leads to the control cabin. You see several people loading the main rescue capsule with scientific gear. You hear one Yazirian scientist say, "Move over! Make room for this box!"

The loudspeaker crackles. "We have entered Volturnian atmosphere and are losing control. Get to your capsules immediately!"

The ship lurches. There's still no sign of Jac. You must make a choice quickly:

1) Get into the Personal Safety Pod by yourself; turn to page 76.

2) Go to your right and join the others getting into the main rescue capsule; turn to page 102.

You can't just give in quietly, you decide. Your dad would want you to protest somehow.

You break the microreader they give you and refuse to eat the food they bring. Each time someone comes to your room, you try to escape through the door.

Finally you fight just one time too many. A Yazirian, two Kurabanda, the Dralasite, and the human all come to your room. Several hold you while one removes all your belongings from your pouches.

"Now, march!" the human demands. "If you can't behave here, maybe you can down below."

Again you walk many corridors, but this time they are not beautiful. They are dull, dark, and damp. You must be going deeper and deeper into the hills.

"You've got only yourself to blame," says the human as he shoves you into a small cell and slams the door. You quickly run to the door and look through the small peephole.

The human looks at you coldly, then turns away and stalks off. You sense a certain finality in his attitude.

Well, you've made your protest, and look where it landed you. You are stuck in a tiny dungeonlike cell, but at least you're certain that your father will soon come looking for you on Volturnus.

THE END

The leaflike things appear to be sturdy. Though thick and leathery-looking, they're light enough to be blown by the wind.

You watch the wind pick up a leaf. It floats until the wind dies, then drifts down again.

A leaf floats toward you. Quickly you leap onto it. At first the leaf sags under your weight, but then the wind lifts it again, and soon you are sailing across the open plain.

You raise your head and look back. The gray Dralasite is hopping up and down, waving its pistol in the air. You faintly hear, "Come back! Come back!"

You settle down to enjoy the strange flight. Ahead, you see other leaves losing their lift over increasingly rough ground. As the wind dies, the leaves fall abruptly to the surface below.

Not wanting to fall, you look around to see where you can jump off. Your eyes widen as you see a group of grazing dinosaurs!

Then you remember the study you made of Volturnus before the trip. They aren't dinosaurs. They're called lopers, and they have been domesticated by some of the natives, called the Ul-Mor.

Hey! Maybe you can ride one.

Still holding Ting in one hand, you jump, hoping you can land without hurting your already sore shoulder. You land rolling and quickly rise to your feet.

The lopers pay no attention to you. You approach them slowly, talking quietly.

You pick some grass and hold it out to a nearby animal. "Here, fella. Good grass."

As you hold the grass out, you pat the large animal with your hand. It inspects you and the grass. Continuing to pat and talk quietly, you walk along its side and place a foot on its big back leg. Then you climb the bony plates that jut from the animal's spine and swing your leg over the loper's back.

The loper doesn't seem to object to your being on its back, but how do you get it to go? You lean back, twiddling your fingers along its spine, thinking about what to do. Suddenly the animal starts moving. It quickly speeds into a ground-covering lope.

You realize that you'd better think about where you're going. Far to your left, you see a cloud of dust. Squinting, you see a herd of animals. Ahead of you the land rises into rocky foothills. You think you see a village of some sort.

1) If you think there might be a helpful herder with the animals, turn to page 39.

2) If you want to go into the hills and look for a village, turn to page 70.

"Wait a minute. Surveyors would be on salary. They wouldn't have to wait to get paid." You decide not to trust them.

There are scraping sounds, and then a human voice says, "Okay, these mineral samples are packed for the Sathar agent."

"What do you think he'll pay for keeping the information from Universal Minerals?"

"More than Universal was going to pay us, that's for sure!" laughs the human voice. "Universal will never know about these minerals. The Sathar will have them before Universal even finds out they were here."

"They can't do that!" you think.

The first voice speaks again. "Radio the Sathar agent that the samples are here. Be sure to tell them to bring enough explosives to bring the whole desert down into these caves, so all they'll have to do is process the rubble. Then we'll check the survey markers. We'll have to be able to answer the agent's questions about the minerals."

"We've got to stop them, Kyiki!" Arnla exclaims. "But how can we do it?"

1) "We can try to reach the radio and broadcast a message to my father." If this is your choice, turn to page 60.

2) "Or maybe it would be quicker to try to get help from the Ul-Mor." If this is your choice, turn to page 107.

You turn toward the mountains, which still seem far off, but you are hopeful, because you have heard your father mention how many mining surveyors are on Volturnus. They must be spread all around. Surely you can find help, maybe where you see a thin plume of smoke in the distance.

You walk on under the warm Volturnian sun, which is high in the greenish sky. As the land begins to get hillier and rougher, you wish you had a loper to ride—especially when you see bright flashes in the foothills off to your left. You are tempted to investigate them.

As you look ahead to the land where you hope to find help, you realize you have a choice.

1) You can go up into the high mountain ahead of you, toward where you see smoke; turn to page 36.

2) Or you can go around the base of the mountain. Maybe those flashes are coming from a river; turn to page 132.

"I would like to see Volturnus," you say. "After all, that's what this field trip was all about. But my folks will get pretty worried about us when they hear that the ship crashed. So we had better stay around here. Help could be on the way right now."

"Sound reasoning, Kyiki." Jac thinks for a moment. "Shall we explore a bit right here, near the pod? Perhaps we can get some value from the trip, after all. I'll be happy to elucidate what we see."

"But if they send a rescue ship, a ground-to-orbit shuttle could drop down for us very quickly. What if we weren't here and it went away again? I think we'd better stay put."

"Wise thinking, young one," Jac says. He folds his many legs, relaxes against the PSP, and pulls a microreader from his pocket. "And I have here some educational riddles that you can answer while we wait."

Is there a difference between educational riddles and a quiz? you wonder. You settle down to wait for the rescue from Volturnus that you are certain will come soon.

THE END

"You're right, Jac," you say. "It might be dangerous to split up now. Let's stay here. We can build a smoky fire to signal anyone in the vicinity."

You and the Vrusk collect lots of wood, some of it damp. Jac uses his Everflame to ignite the woodpile. The fire trickles along the sticks, looking as if it's more likely to burn out than to burst into flame.

As you watch, the entire woodpile bursts into a giant bonfire. Before you can control the fire, sparks ignite nearby trees.

You, Jac, and Pongo move to the open plain and watch, appalled, as the beautiful woods burns. Little boxlike creatures scurry by, honking angrily.

Suddenly, above the sound of the fire, you hear a different roar. You look up and see an approaching space shuttle.

But right now your attention is claimed by the fire.

"When I saw the burned woods in the future, I didn't know we would cause it," you say sadly.

"Even when we see the future, we don't always make the right decisions, Kyiki."

"Yeah. And now the right decision has to be to get home on the shuttle. But I wish we could see into the future enough to know whether the ship is going to get us home safely or take us into even more trouble."

THE END

You realize that you don't know this strange planet at all. Arnla has lived on Volturnus all her life and she has probably visited lots of places.

As you were taken from the mound, her expression looked sympathetic. You're certain she would help you again if you could reach her.

You have no problem following the tracks left by the loper on its journey back to the Ul-Mor village. After about an hour, you notice a little dust cloud on the horizon. It looks much like the cloud you saw when you spotted Arnla's kwidge herd.

"Uh-oh," you say to yourself. "If I can see the herd, probably the herder can see me." You notice that one plume of dust is moving toward you.

You realize your danger, but there's nowhere to run and nowhere to hide. Besides, you are still far from the Ul-Mor village, so what could they punish you for? You decide to wait for whatever will happen. Gradually the dust comes nearer and you see that it's a loper. Then you recognize that there's an Ul-Mor on the loper.

Then the loper prances up to you and you see that it's Arnla!

The Ul-Mor girl's eyes light with joy as she reins in the loper and reaches out with her mind-link tentacle. You feel the coolness of the tentacle on your neck.

"Oh, Kyiki. I'm so glad I found you. The

council was so unfair!" Her eyes snap in anger.

"No, Arnla. They weren't unfair. Sure, I don't like being left in the middle of nowhere without food or water. But your law says that water is sacred and must not be taken except in a ceremony."

"I know you are a good human. And I still want to help you."

"But, Arnla, won't you get in trouble?" you ask.

"Trouble? No. The herd will stay where it is. And when we part, if you give me something of yours that I can say I stole, I'll get credit for that."

That still seems a little strange to you, but so much of Volturnus has been strange that it doesn't matter.

"Okay. But where can we go? I still need to find help so I can get home."

"I think we have to go toward the rising sun. Some humans we saw recently were going that way. But we have a lot of desert to cross, which will be very uncomfortable, even riding my loper. We could go into the caves below the desert, where it is cooler and water is available. But the caves are very dangerous."

"After one experience of being really thirsty on Volturnus, I think I'd rather stay near water."

"All right," Arnla agrees, "but I don't know what we'll find." She releases Quin-Quin and takes you to a huge mound of big rocks that you had passed a while before. You hadn't dreamed that they hid the opening to a cool, moist cave.

As you drop into a sloping tunnel, you realize that it is not entirely natural. Someone—or something—has smoothed the sides. But before you can start to worry about that, the tunnel opens into a large passageway.

At first you can see by the light coming through the hole, but when you turn a corner, darkness surrounds you.

"Wait a minute, Arnla. We need light. Let's see what I've got with me." You dig into your belt pouch until you feel a short, flashlight-shaped object. You take the microreader from the pouch, remove the magnifying glass from its end, and turn it on. Its beam lights up the ceiling.

"Okay, let's go," you say.

You walk together, Arnla in mind-link with you, the little microreader dimly lighting the way. Occasionally you hear a small animal scurry for cover.

"What's that?" Arnla asks abruptly.

"Where?"

"There, along the wall."

You shine the light toward where Arnla is pointing. "It's a rope, made from vines." Your voice drops to a whisper. "Someone must have made it. They might still be here!"

Now you proceed more cautiously. Little animals that Arnla calls rasties chitter at you but run from your light. In one room you see

the peels from a fruit you don't recognize. In another is a box that appears to have contained ammunition.

As you turn another corner in the corridor, you stop without warning.

"What is it?" Arnla asks, puzzled.

"Can you smell that musty smell? And something like flowers, too? That's odd."

You walk on carefully. The smell gets stronger, and gradually you realize the corridor is getting brighter. You think you hear humming and singing. At the next bend in the corridor, you hear a voice singing: "Just you wait till the next snipe hunt. I'll get you; I'll get you."

Whatever you are smelling and hearing is just around the corner. You hold Arnla back and carefully peer into the gloom.

You see a large monkeylike figure seated against the wall, a laser pistol lying nearby. The creature is twirling a twig in fingers with odd round pads on them.

Suddenly it grabs the pistol, jumps to its feet, and looks down the corridor. Then, in one swift motion, it turns to face you.

You jump back quickly. It must not have seen you, because in a minute it resumes singing.

"I'm guarding my front; I'm guarding my back. Oh, just wait till the snipe hunt comes!"

You feel Arnla's thoughts. "The guard is a Kurabanda. He must be working for someone. Maybe you'll be able to get help from them."

"I'm not sure I'd want to trust someone who needs a guard," you say.

"What shall we do?" she asks.

1) "We can go back out and cross the desert instead." Turn to page 92.

2) "We can try to trick the guard into leaving its post." Turn to page 54.

You know your captors are not fools. They're going to listen to every word you say and not let you get away with anything. You're probably going to get hurt if you try to say anything to your dad that you shouldn't.

"Yes, Dad. It's me. I'm on Vol—" A hand quickly slaps over your mouth.

"Just read the paper, kid. Nothing more!" Gorlo growls in your ear.

You hold the paper up and read.

"'Your child, Kyiki, is safe. Kyiki will remain safe as long as you follow these instructions. Send all of the information your surveyors have gathered about possible mining sites on Volturnus. In addition, send a thousand kilograms of gold and a hundred kilos of diamonds. Send the ship to the edge of the large desert on Volturnus, near the mountains. We will contact you there.'"

"But what about you, Kyiki?" he interrupts.

"I'll be all right, Dad. Just follow the directions they gave you." You're supposed to stop there, but you can't resist adding, "Please, Dad, get me out of here, but don't take any chances." Then the hand returns to your mouth and another hand yanks you out of the chair.

"Get back to your room, kid. We don't need you anymore," Gorlo demands gruffly.

You return to your room and try not to build up any false hopes of being rescued.

A few restless days later, the ransom arrives. You are taken out into an open area, not far from where you originally crashed, and left there. Gorlo tells you as he leaves, "Don't worry. Someone will come for you soon."

After waiting an hour, afraid to move from that spot, you hear the sound of a shuttle arriving. It's a Universal Minerals shuttle! And your father is on board. As you prepare to see him, you wonder if you should have tried to do something that would have prevented your father from having to give away his secrets and his gold.

THE END

"A rescue shuttle could come anytime. We need to see it because it might not stay and look for us. Let's explore right nearby."

"That's logical, Kyiki," says your tutor.

You are in an open, grassy area. You look in all directions. To your left are a few low trees and some rocks. The greenery gives way to desert, and far off, you see the dark shapes of either clouds or mountains.

Little seems worth seeing. But you notice that there are more and more trees.

"Let's go over there and look around," you say, pointing to a nearby woods.

The two of you set off toward the woods, the Vrusk moving slowly to let you keep up.

"I'm sure we'll be back here," says Jac. "So you might as well leave Ting."

You're reluctant, but you agree.

You near the wooded area. It looks cool and comforting, although there's something puzzling about the trees. They seem to shimmer, as if they were about to disappear.

You stop short as a motion catches your eye. Before you is a patch of low-growing plants with large, dangling, blue crystals instead of flowers. A small blue creature shaped like a box with legs trundles over to one of the plants and begins to nibble the crystal with a faint crunching sound.

"Fascinating!" Jac whispers. You wait for an explanation, but none comes.

Please turn to page 146.

You know these guys aren't going to let you get away with much. There's too much at stake. Maybe you can at least work in a clue that will help your dad. But what?

The radio crackles and you hear your father's voice say excitedly, "Kyiki? Is that you? Where are you?"

"Just read the paper, kid," Gorlo says.

But you can't just give in.

"Volturnus, Dad. I'm in an old Eorna complex in the foothills. Please, Da—" A hand slaps over your mouth and an angry Gorlo hauls you out of the chair.

As you're dragged out of the room, you hear Sparks say into the radio, "You heard your kid. Now, listen. Here's what we want you to do. . . ."

You're dragged down corridor after corridor. Finally Gorlo stops.

As the Dralasite opens the door into a dark cell, it says, "You shot it all, kid. You're too much trouble. We'll just have to find a way to get what we want without you."

Gorlo throws you into the cell. Then it takes out a gun and raises the weapon over its head. From the floor, you watch the gun descend as you hear Gorlo say, "Sleep well, kid. You should have listened."

THE END

"We can't just sit and wait! The beacon probably isn't telling anyone anything."

"Have you considered all possibilities, Kyiki?" Ting asks a little sternly.

Your eye is caught by your combination radio-calculator on your wrist. "My chronocom just isn't powerful enough to send a signal all the way out of the atmosphere."

You sit down on the ground, thinking and looking vaguely around. Then something else catches your eye—a broken tree branch.

"A fire!" you exclaim. "I'll build a signal fire. Anyone nearby will see it."

"Good, Kyiki. Think first, then act."

You set to work collecting all the dead branches you can find. You pile the wood the way you learned in Cadets. You stuff dried grass into the pile and then hold your pocket firecell above the grass. The light of the Volturnian sun is concentrated by the yellow crystals of the firecell. Soon smoke begins to wisp out of the pile. If anyone is around, they'll see the smoke.

You sit in the shade of your PSP, nibbling on some dried food you found on the craft. You take off your chronocom. Activating it, you speak into the tiny radio: "This is Kyiki. Testing." You don't expect any response, but the tiny device crackles and you hear, "We hear you. Is that your signal fire? Stay there. We're coming."

"Did you hear, Ting? Help is coming!"

"Think twice, Kyiki!"

"You're always saying that!"

Soon you see a skimmer speeding toward you. The skimmer pulls up and hovers next to your PSP. A large, fierce-looking human gets out. Two Yazirians stay inside.

"Anyone with you?" the man demands.

"No, sir. I escaped from a spaceship that was falling into the atmosphere. I was all alone in the rescue pod."

"Okay. Get in the skimmer. We'll find out who you are and what we can do with you."

You don't like the way he said that, but you don't seem to have much choice. You grab Ting and start to enter the hovercar.

"What's the box, kid?" one of the Yazirians asks gruffly.

"My Compu-Pal," you say, but you don't want them to know any more.

"We'll just relieve you of that burden." It grabs Ting and flings your computer friend back into the pod.

"Blast!" you say angrily to yourself. "It didn't have to do that!" And you jerk your shoulder from the human's grasp.

The hovercar lifts up on its cushion of air and zooms away from your PSP. You wonder why you don't feel you've been rescued.

You watch the land change from black, sandy desert to orange fields. Occasionally you glimpse small green wooded areas. Then, in the middle of nowhere, the hovercar stops.

"Get out. Perhaps you will be able to find a friend here."

-ROSLOF

Mystified, you get out and see a small tent. Two walls split and out comes a large, shiny brown, eight-legged creature.

"Jac!"

"Kyiki! I thought you were dead. I was remiss in not making certain you were safe."

"You can talk all you want later. Get in that tent and stay there until we return!" The human pushes you through the opening. Soon the roar of the skimmer disappears into the distance. You and your tutor are alone.

"Who are they, Jac?" you whisper.

"You needn't whisper, Kyiki. They've left me alone before, but there was no point in my leaving until I had some idea of where I am. I don't know who they are. Whenever I ask questions, they reply that someone will be along soon to take care of me."

"Take care of you? Do they mean—like gangsters?" you ask, your eyes wide.

"You watch too much video, Kyiki."

Parting the tent flap, you peer out.

"No one's out there, Jac. Let's go out and look around." You slip through the opening, half expecting to be stopped.

You and Jac walk all around the tent, looking in every direction. Behind the tent, about a thousand meters away, you see the edge of what might be a forest.

"Let's head over there, Jac. Maybe we can find out what's going on around here."

Please turn to page 146.

"Knowing we can visit other times is great, Jac, but I don't think we should leave this time period. Rescue might come at any moment, and if we're not here, they won't know where to look for us. Besides, what if we can't get back?"

"All right, Kyiki. I suppose you're right," the tutor says glumly.

You and Jac continue exploring the camp. Pongo sticks close to you.

You keep returning to the locked hut, as if trying the door over and over would make it open. After one try, you notice that Pongo is very still. His head is tilted to one side, as if listening intently. You listen and hear a low roar in the distance.

"What's that noise, Jac?" you ask. As the Vrusk listens, the roar gets louder.

Looking out over the grassy plain, you see a cloud of dust.

As the dust cloud draws nearer, you see that it is caused by a group of skimmers moving in a line. One is larger and appears to have a great deal of storage space.

"Hide, Kyiki!" Jac urges. You and Jac quickly duck behind a clump of bushes.

The vehicles stop at the edge of the woods. Doors open and out pour at least fifteen occupants—humans, Yazirians, a large Vrusk, and even two Dralasites

One Yazirian seems to be the leader. It angrily orders the others to unload the largest vehicle.

If anyone seems too slow, the Yazirian lashes out with its whip. The tips of the whip give off electric sparks, which seem to stun the victims.

"What are we going to do?" you whisper.

"We'd better leave before they finish unloading," Jac says. He keeps his long body as low as possible and begins to slither into the woods, with you right behind.

Suddenly a green furry shape jumps out of a tree and lands on top of you, screeching in glee. It's Pongo!

"Catch them!" you hear the leader shriek.

You try to run, but now Pongo is hanging around your waist, making it difficult to keep up with Jac.

A black thing snakes past you in the air. The leader's whip! It strikes the Vrusk in the legs, and he goes down, entangled in the whip. He shudders in pain as the electric thongs penetrate even his hard shell.

You see a small sphere soar past you. It breaks against a tree, and a cloud spreads through the air. You try to stop, but you're too . . . late . . . .

You wake to find yourself in a small dark shack. Jac lies beside you, and Pongo is curled up by your head. You start to move but stop abruptly when you hear a voice.

"Thu-ju Kip sure can be a stinker," a high-pitched voice complains.

"Yeah," agrees another voice, "but I'll put up with him for a while. I don't know any

other way to earn so much so quickly. So I'll be a pirate until I have enough money to set myself up for life."

Pirates! No wonder they didn't want you wandering around their camp.

"You say that now, but you haven't been hit by that stinker's whip yet," the high-pitched voice says.

"And I won't be, either! I'll do everything Thu-ju Kip says. I'll guard this kid and the Vrusk, just like he told me."

Jac stirs slightly. You reach over and touch him on the shoulder. His eyes open and he sees you holding your finger to your lips. He nods, understanding.

The voice continues outside your door. "That stuff from the cargo ship will make us all rich. And you've got to admit that it was clever of Thu-Ju Kip to have us go the long way around—the cargo ship crew had it all unloaded before we got there."

The unseen speaker laughs and adds, "I'm just glad we get to guard the kid and Vrusk. That cargo ship's crew is plenty mad."

"What shall we do?" you whisper urgently.

"It appears we have two choices, Kyiki.

1) "We could just stay put and not cause any trouble. Maybe they'll let us go." Turn to page 126.

2) "Or we could try to escape and reach the time machine." Turn to page 62.

"You're right, Ting. That creature is just too big and ferocious-looking." And you turn to the priest. "I just can't fight that thing," you say.

"That is your decision," the priest says, standing straight and acting very official. "You will remain here among the Edestekai. You will work each day in the fields, helping to grow morda and arbon as food for the village. You will be given enough food to guarantee that you can live and work. Give me that box that talks, please. You will no longer need it."

The spidery priest removes Ting from your hands, and you realize that you have chosen to be a slave. As you are led out of the temple, you see that all your future holds is work . . . and the hope that someday your father will free you.

THE END

"Hey, Ting. Mines mean mountains, right? So we'll most likely find mining surveyors up on a mountain."

As you climb higher and higher, the going becomes rougher and you stumble frequently, always trying to protect Ting when you fall.

"Is this banging around absolutely necessary, Kyiki?" Ting asks complainingly.

Wisps of smoke or fog drift past your face, until gradually you realize that you are walking into thick smog and can see only a few feet ahead of you. Some of the black mists have an evil, oily smell.

"I guess I was wrong, Ting. We'll go back down." As you speak, you take one more step into the black mist . . . and you fall into the fiery pit of a live volcano. Now you will never leave Volturnus.

THE END

"I think one of us should stay near the pod and the other should go see if there's help somewhere," you say.

Jac looks thoughtful. "I probably shouldn't let you go off on your own. I'm responsible. But this is supposed to be an educational field trip. Let's make it a test of how wise and responsible you can be. Do you have your compass?"

"Yes."

"Which way will you head?" asks Jac.

"Well, when we came here from the ship, I thought I saw some smoke or dust over in the other direction. I think I'll go back that way."

You and Jac walk back to the Personal Safety Pod. You check in your pouch to see what you have that might be useful. You decide to take Ting, your Compu-Pal.

You're excited and frightened as you say good-bye to your tutor. What a field trip this is turning out to be!

The billow of smoke or dust still rises over the horizon, where you saw it before. You set out across the open dry land toward it.

You walk for almost an hour, seemingly making no progress. But then you think you see strange shapes through the dust. You squint your eyes and—yes! Animals! A whole herd of animals!

Please turn to page 39.

ROSLOF

Nearing the herd, you see that they are large birds! They have orange, pointed beaks, featherless heads with yellow and red markings, round green bodies, and tiny wings. Chippering busily, they chase each other playfully, often trying—always unsuccessfully—to fly. Some birds, probably mothers, make harsh noises at the little ones.

You watch, fascinated, and then notice a movement on a rock near the herd.

You blink, fearing you are seeing things. But they're still there. A plum-colored octopus wearing a green feathery headdress sits on a rock. By the rock lies a green lizardlike animal with spikes jutting from its spine. One of the octopus's tentacles lies across the green animal's neck.

"Let's get out of here," you say to Ting.

At that moment the octopus sees you. It leaps from the rock to the lizard's back.

You turn to run, but a tentacle grabs you around the waist. You push at the octopus's head as the thing draws you toward it. Another tentacle—smooth, dry, and kind of tickling—worms into your shirt. You feel a strange coolness on your back and . . .

"Don't be afraid."

You feel a voice inside your head. Someone else's mind is touching yours. You can relax—the octopus is friendly.

"Ul-Mor are not octopuses. We have nine tentacles. That makes me a novepus. I use my ninth tentacle to talk with you. Understand?"

You don't understand, and the novepus seems to know that. It removes its tentacle and you no longer feel its mind communicating with yours. When the tentacle returns, you feel the knifelike coolness and know you are linked to the strange creature again.

"Who are you?" you ask aloud, forgetting the fact that your thoughts can be heard.

You feel the novepus answer through the mind-link. "My name is Arnla-Kon. My tribe of Ul-Mor lives near here."

"Do you all talk through your tentacle?"

"We can hear anything you say. When we talk together we use sounds that only the Ul-Mor can understand. But with anything else, yes, we communicate through mind-link."

That could get embarrassing, you think.

"Only if you want to lie or think bad thoughts," you feel Arnla answer.

"What are these birds?" you ask quickly, to avoid further embarrassment.

"Kwidges," she answers. "Usually a male takes care of the kwidges because herding is very important work. But I don't like taking care of houses and babies, so the elders agreed to let me herd sometimes."

"Hey, that's great!" you say.

"What I really like is riding Quin-Quin." She pats her saddled dinosaurlike animal. "This is my loper, Quin-Quin."

"Ahem!" you hear from Ting's case.

"Ting!" you exclaim, surprised at having forgotten. "Arnla, meet Ting, my Compu-Pal."

"How do you do, Arnla-Kon?" Ting says. "May I ask how you ride Quin-Quin?"

"We use the mind-link with the lopers and just let their minds know what to do. But, Kyiki, how did you—and Ting—get here?"

You explain your predicament and add, "I HAVE to find a way to get home!"

"I'll help you!" Arnla says excitedly.

"Great! Can you help me find some radio equipment to radio my father?"

"The Ul-Mor don't have radios, but our elders see many strange creatures from other planets. Maybe the elders will help." Her warm smile fades. "But maybe they won't. They don't like strangers. What do you want to do?"

"Uh, er, Arnla? Would you—?"

"Cut our mind-link while you think?" she finishes for you, laughing.

"Yes, please." You feel red-faced.

1) If you want to go with Arnla to the Ul-Mor village and perhaps get help there, turn to page 112.

2) If you don't trust the strange creatures, despite Arnla's friendliness, head for the mountains alone; turn to page 86.

As Kyiki, you certainly wouldn't be allowed near the broadcast equipment. But as the Boss, it's a different story.

All you have to do is stay away from guards who may know of the Boss's absence.

You don the holobelt and insert the disc in place so that it is drawing power from the belt and not using up its own power.

This is going to be tricky, you think as you start out. You've got to hit a balance between moving cautiously in order to avoid the guards and moving confidently to convince anyone seeing you that you are the real Boss.

You make your way through the complex. Several times you pass open doors of rooms with guards in them. Each time you hold your breath as you pass, but no one calls out.

Reaching the radio room, you listen carefully at the door but hear nothing. You draw a deep breath and open the door.

Right inside the room, facing you, is a Kurabanda, busy cleaning the room.

"Sparks has gone to lunch, sir," it says.

"That's all right," you say in what you hope is a deep adult voice. "I just got back and I need to contact the Sathar."

"Yes, sir. You go ahead. I'll finish up in here later," it says and leaves.

Quickly you pull out your personal radio key and insert it into the slot in the big crystal structure.

Instantly you hear, "Kyiki?"

"It's me, Dad. I've got to be quick. I'm on

Volturnus, in an old Eorna complex in the low hills near the desert."

"I've got our new map right in front of me. The surveyors didn't find the Eorna complex, but I've heard stories about a beautiful underground city. . . ."

"That's it! I think there's only about twenty people in the gang here. They get their orders from somewhere else."

"Probably the Sathar," he says, thinking. "Okay, Kyiki. We'll come ready for anything. Starting in about six hours, I want you to stay in your room, preferably under cover. Stay there until you hear from me. Good work, youngster. I'm proud of you."

The afternoon is very long. Toward evening you settle into your room. You'd like to watch what happens, but you promised your father that you would wait for him.

It isn't long before sounds begin to reach your ears—running footsteps, shouts of confusion, the occasional zap of a laser rifle, thunderous crashes.

Finally all is quiet. Still you stay where you are.

"Kyiki?" you hear a faint voice call.

You scramble out of your safe corner and go to the door.

"Dad?" you shout. And there he is, wrapping you in his arms.

"Come on, Kyiki. Let's go home!"

THE END

You think a moment. "I don't think we could reach the cargo ship with all those pirates moving around. They'd see us."

"Do you think you could get us to a time just a little earlier?" asks Jac.

"Sure," you say. "Let's go!"

You turn the knob again, making sure you zoom past the dangerous time but then slow down as you enter the unknown.

When you open your eyes, you look around and see emptiness. No camp. No strangers. And there's no sign that anyone has ever visited the area.

Then, in the distance, you hear a roaring sound that quickly grows. The roar turns to a whistle as a red spaceship appears in the sky. As it flashes overhead, you see that it is flat and square in shape. There are many windows along each of the straight sides, and you catch the glint of sunlight flashing off lenses, perhaps telescopes.

One of the lenses moves slightly and seems to focus on you.

Suddenly the whine of the ship's engine changes pitch and the huge red ship swoops down like a blown leaf. The sound cuts out and the ship settles gently to the ground, less than a kilometer away.

You watch as a panel on the side of the ship opens. A ramp swings out, and a large ball-shaped object rolls down the ramp. It hesitates, changes direction, and then rolls toward your platform.

You and Jac watch, fascinated. You've seen pictures of these old ships in history books, but you never thought you'd see one outside a museum. The ball stops a meter or so from the platform, then splits in half, revealing a spherical Dralasite.

The creature rolls up to you and says in a high-pitched voice, "Human? Vrusk?"

You and Jac both nod.

"What are you doing here? We have just chosen this planet as next to be developed. Nowhere in our files does it say that aliens have been here. You are facts that cannot be explained by what we know of Volturnus. Therefore, you must not be here!" As he talks, his ball-shaped body gradually develops a foot, which he stamps in anger.

"We'd rather NOT be here," you say, and you explain about your ship crashing.

The Dralasite thinks for a moment and then says impatiently, "Come. We'll take you to your home. Then you won't be here and we won't have to explain your presence. We cannot be held responsible for your being here. You have to be somewhere else."

You and Jac happily agree and you walk to the ship and up the ramp. The red doors slide shut behind you.

You will soon be somewhere else—home and safe.

THE END

You realize that it's just too dangerous to use the holodisc. You have no idea how many guards know that the Boss is gone. Besides, your father has been called. By now he is probably on his way. It would be safer both for him and you to just stay and wait.

You turn off the disc and remove the holo-belt. Reluctantly, you hide them under your bed, planning to return them to the storeroom after things quiet down.

A few hours later you walk casually into the lounge, trying hard to look as if nothing had happened.

A Kurabanda says, "But Polurd is certain he saw the Boss in the hallway!"

"Couldn't have been," a human says. The Boss is with the Sathar and won't be back till tomorrow."

You pretend very hard not to be listening. But inside you are thanking your stars you decided not to use that holodisc.

Just then the door bursts open and Gorlo appears. "On your feet, men. The Boss just called. The special holodisc is missing, and we've got orders to find whoever is using it. Every square centimeter of this place is to be searched."

The guards run from the room, leaving you alone. You've got to get that thing out of your room!

You leave the lounge and go down the hall toward your room. Ahead of you, a Dralasite goes into a room while a Yazirian goes into another room across the hall. You know they will be busy searching for a few minutes. You might just have time.

The corridor is clear as you round the corner by your room. You reach under the bed. The belt and disc are still there. You have only a few minutes before the guards will get to your room. You have to do something!

There's no real reason why you might not have a holobelt in your room. So that can stay there. The disc is the problem. In fact, it should be back in the storeroom.

Putting the disc in your pouch, you go back out into the corridor. It's empty, so you walk toward the storeroom. You're only a few feet away when the door to the storeroom opens and Gorlo walks out.

"It isn't there," Gorlo calls over its shoulder. "The special drawer is empty!"

You're too late! There's no point in trying to get it back into the drawer now. But what should you do with it?

Just then two guards come out of a room and head down the corridor. An idea pops into your head. Maybe you can get rid of this hot potato.

You creep up behind the two guards as they walk. Quickly you set the timed delay switch on the disc and attach it to the back of the human guard. Then you turn and move quietly back to your room.

Now to wait for the confusion that is sure to follow soon.

You search your room for all your important belongings. With luck you won't be in this room again. Then you stand behind the open door, listening.

"There's the imposter!" someone shouts. It's worked. The holodisc has switched on and now the guard looks like the Boss.

You hear the sound of footsteps running from all directions.

Now's the time to move! You walk calmly through the hallways, past guards scurrying in all directions. Finally you reach the corridor that leads to the exit from the underground complex.

And then you see one more guard, a Kurabanda. It's guarding the exit door! Thinking quickly, you run up to it and tug on its gun belt. Your other hand holds the Stunstick that you've had hidden away all these days.

"Quick! The Boss's imposter has been seen! We've got to get him!" you say excitedly.

"What?" The guard looks puzzled. "But I'm not supposed—"

"Hurry!" you interrupt. "The Boss has been contacted. He says everyone is needed for the search!"

That does it. The guard grabs its rifle and runs down the corridor you just left. The instant you see the Kurabanda round a corner, you move to the door.

Quickly you're through the door and into the rocks. You take a moment to move a couple of boulders against the door, hoping that their weight will delay the guards when they discover you're gone.

As you make your way down the hillside to the smoother land below, you hear a noise. It's a space shuttle, coming in to land. You recognize the shape of the shuttle—it belongs to Universal Minerals.

As you run, you try to figure out where the shuttle will land. Suddenly you trip and fall head forward on the rocky hillside. You lie there, gasping to regain your breath. As you lie there, you hear pounding on the door that you blocked with rocks. You're afraid that the kidnappers will get out, see the shuttle, and get there first.

Before your breath is totally back, you rise to your feet and start to make your way down the hill again. As you move, your lungs gradually stop heaving and fill once more.

You run across the open plain at the base of the hill. The shuttle has landed in a small, smooth area. Raising your left wrist, you flick the little switch of your chronocom to "Broadcast."

"Hello! Hello, Universal Minerals. If you're listening, this is Kyiki. I can see the shuttle." You stumble and gasp. "Please let me in! They're after me!" You don't know whether anyone has heard you or not.

You hear shouting up on the hillside behind you. You push your legs even faster.

Using the chronocom again, you say, "Hello, shuttle. Please open the hatch!"

-ROSLOF

A streak of dazzling light zips past your head. They're shooting at you!

As you run, hoping against hope, you look up and see the side of the shuttle opening outward.

"Kyiki!" a figure in the hatchway shouts.

"Dad!"

And you're up the ramp. The door closes behind you as the zing of a laser blast hits it.

Your dad's arm is still tight around your shoulders as he explains. Because you escaped when you did, you've saved all the gold and the information that he would have been forced to give to the enemy.

This has been a field trip you'll never forget!

THE END

"I think I know how we can trick the guard into letting us by," you say gleefully. "It's an old trick, but I bet it'll work."

You feel along the floor for a loose stone, finally finding one about ten centimeters across. The Kurabanda guard is walking back and forth in the corridor, humming to itself.

You wait until it is turned away from you, then you throw the stone into an opening on the far side of the guard's station. It makes a satisfying THUNK and then rolls.

The monkeylike guard stands straight, listening, its pistol forgotten for the moment. It scratches its head and looks all around, waiting for the sound to be repeated.

It finally makes up its mind, raises its pistol, and moves cautiously over to the opening.

Clearly, it doesn't want to go and find out what made the noise. But suddenly it straightens its back, squares its shoulders, and walks quickly into the room where you threw the stone.

You grab Arnla's tentacle and begin to tiptoe past the door. You glance into the opening and see the guard scratching its head in confusion. Then the two of you hurry past the door and around a corner.

Here there are small lights mounted on the walls every few meters. You see many footprints on the floor. At these signs of activity, you and Arnla become even more cautious. You decide to remove your shoes.

At the next corner, you lean against the wall

and take off one shoe. As you're tying it to your belt, you hear another voice coming from somewhere near.

You quickly remove the other shoe and press against the wall, listening carefully to make sure the voices aren't moving toward you.

They seem to be stationary, so you start to move, slowly and carefully, down the hall.

As you near a corner, you hear a human voice say, "These caves couldn't be better for the work we've got to do."

"The records can be kept here until collected." The second voice is like that of the monkeylike creature who was guarding the hall.

"Okay. Let's get this information in shape. The sooner we give them what they want to know about the minerals on Volturnus, the sooner we get paid," the human voice says.

"Oh, good, you can get help now." That was Arnla's thought on your mind-link.

1) If you think these people will help you and you should step out and identify yourself, turn to page 84.

2) If you think you had better continue to listen before you decide, turn to page 11.

You have no desire to challenge a zapgun, and the floating leaves don't look strong enough to hold you.

You decide to just keep walking, as the Dralasite demands. Besides, you really do want to know what this is all about.

"Who are you?" you ask the figure behind you. "And why are you doing this?"

"Because I'm one Dralasite who does a job, and right now my job is getting hold of you in order to get at your father."

"My dad!" you exclaim, swinging around. "What does he have to do with this?"

"Never you mind," says the Dralasite. "Hey! What's that thing you just swung?"

"Oh, nothing!" you say, clutching Ting to you. "It's just a little computer my father gave me to help with my homework."

"Your father, huh? Well, keep it safe. Maybe it'll come in handy."

Relieved that you can keep Ting, you walk on. The ground gradually rises into rough hillsides. Walking becomes more difficult.

Suddenly your foot slips and you sprawl flat, almost losing Ting.

"Get up! And don't try anything funny," the Dralasite demands, jabbing its zapgun into your back.

As you stand up, you look around the huge rock that blocks your path.

Please turn to page 108.

You must forget about your thirst. Arnla said it was a crime to take water because its distribution is a religious ceremony.

You lie on your couch, trying to think of anything that doesn't remind you of your thirst. Instead, you think of forests and waterfalls and the planet Hydros, where you once spent an underwater vacation.

Somehow, the night passes. The dark green sky begins to lighten. Kon-Dudro comes to wake you, carrying a bowl of water, and ceremoniously offers it to you.

"An Ul-Mor good-morning to you. May your day bring the blessings of water from the One Who is Many."

You don't know what that means, but it makes you feel warm and cared for. You take a sip of the cool water and immediately feel as if you have drunk oceans of the refreshing liquid. All your bad dreams of the night are gone, and you feel very much at home.

Arnla comes skipping cheerfully into the mound. "Kyiki! Guess what! The council of elders says you can go herding with me while they debate about you. Won't that be fun?"

You don't know what will happen next or if the council will help you get home. But you're not sure that matters. These Ul-Mor are so nice that you won't mind staying with them on Volturnus for a long time.

THE END

You think about the zapgun. It can be set on blast, which will probably kill you, or on stun, which would knock you out. It's probably on stun, though, because whoever planned your kidnapping seems to want you in one piece.

You decide it's worth taking a chance.

Pretending to stumble, you take off at full speed toward your left.

Behind you, you hear the Dralasite shout.

You lower your head and see your shadow racing along with you. Then the shadow changes shape and becomes a large web of bright splotches and dark lines. It's a tangler grenade!

You feel the many sticky strands of the tangler web surround you. They fall on your head, your shoulders, your back. They wrap around your face, your arms, your legs. You fall to the ground, trapped in an unbreakable web.

"You ARE going with me, you know," the Dralasite says sneeringly. "Get up!"

It uses a small vibroknife to cut a few of the tough strands so your feet can move.

"Now, march!" it orders.

And so you walk, each step made difficult by the sticky strands of the tangler web covering you. When you reach a rocky hillside, the weblike prison is cut away by the Dralasite. As you breathe a sigh of relief, your attention is caught by the rocks.

Please turn to page 108.

"Hmmmm. That guy just mentioned radioing to the Sathar. If we can get to the equipment, I know how to use it." You're only exaggerating a little—you used your father's radio equipment exactly once.

The voices fade away in the distance. There must be another exit up ahead.

"We've got to be sure no one else is here, Kyiki," Arnla reminds you.

Holding one of Arnla's tentacles tightly, you begin to move again, very quietly. After several minutes, you've still heard nothing. It's beginning to look as if no one is left in the caves.

Then, as you creep down the corridor, you hear a voice droning nearby, occasionally punctuated by a crackle of static. You turn a corner and see light coming from several rooms. One room, brighter than the others, is where the voice is coming from.

"That's all. We'll wait for the agent's pickup at six o'clock tomorrow. Over and out." You hear the sound of the machine being clicked off.

You back swiftly around the corner and out of sight. You hear footsteps enter the corridor and then gradually fade away.

You take Arnla's arm again and cautiously inch toward the radio room.

"Careful, Kyiki," you feel her whisper.

SCRE-E-E-CH!

You stop so abruptly that Arnla slides into you and wraps herself around your leg.

You signal her to be quiet, forgetting that you are far more likely to make noise.

You hear a cough, followed by another screech of a chair being moved on rock.

There must be another guard in the radio room!

"Wow! I'm sure glad we were being careful. We might have blundered into that guard!" you exclaim silently, knowing that the mind-link will tell Arnla what you're saying.

"Where did it come from?" Arnla asks.

"It must have been in there all the time."

"How can we get to the radio?"

"I've got a Stunstick. Uncle Kloss gave it to me for my last birthday. I promised him I wouldn't use it on people, but he didn't know I was going to get stuck on a strange planet with dangerous people."

"Would it kill the guard, Kyiki?"

"No. It would just shock it into being quiet for a while."

"Is there another way?"

"Well . . . we could try to trick it somehow, but I don't know if we could keep it away long enough to radio my dad and find a place to hide while we wait to be rescued."

1) If you want to try to trick the guard, turn to page 151.

2) If you want to attack the guard, turn to page 100.

"Somehow we've got to get to the time machine again," you whisper decisively.

Suddenly your anger at being helpless makes you bold, and you decide you want to see your captors. Moving to the doorway, you lift the cloth flap and look out.

"Hello," you say to the guards. One is a Dralasite and the other a human, only a few years older than you.

"Hey, the kid's awake," the human says.

"About time," says the Dralasite in the high-pitched voice. "What's your name, kid?"

"Kyiki. And this is Jac, my tutor."

"Tutor!" That seems to strike the human as hilarious. He roars with laughter.

"You find THAT funny? You don't know a good joke when you hear one!" the Dralasite complains, then turns back to you.

"You might as well settle back down, kid. Our leader is busy right now, unloading stuff we kinda borrowed from a cargo ship."

"Are you really pirates?" you ask.

"None of your business, kid!" the Dralasite says gruffly.

There's a moment of silence, then the Dralasite says in a friendlier tone, "Hey, kid. Do you know any good jokes?"

"Jokes?" you ask, puzzled. Then you begin to get an idea. "Sure, I know lots of them."

"Tell me some," begs the Dralasite.

Your mind spins until you remember a riddle your sister asked you recently. "Okay. When is a door not a door?"

"I said GOOD jokes!" growls the Dralasite. "When it's ajar, of course. That one is old, old, old!"

"I know some better ones," you say.

"Sure you do, kid," snarls the Dralasite. "That's why you told me a lousy one, huh?"

"I've got an idea," you say. "I'll tell you three jokes. If I get you to laugh, you let us out of here."

"Out? You gotta be kidding!" exclaims the human, who has been listening.

"Wait, Carson," says the Dralasite. "Why not? If they're all as awful as that last one, we can't lose. Okay, kid. Make me laugh and you and that giant bug get out."

You feel Jac stir in anger and turn to silently beg him to let the insult go.

Every joke you ever heard spins through your mind in a mad jumble. "Okay, here's the first one. Why don't Earth people go to the moon for their vacations?"

"Why? Why?" the Dralasite demands.

"Because it has no atmosphere." You hold your breath in the silence that follows your answer. And then you hear a chuckle.

"Hey, that's not bad, kid. Not great, but not bad, either. What's next?"

"What do you do with a green monster?"

The Dralasite thinks a minute and then says, "I give up."

"Wait till it ripens!" you shout.

The Dralasite doesn't seem to react. Then the gray, claylike mass of its body begins to quiver uncontrollably. Finally, a large, hearty laugh erupts from the guard.

Eager to finish this strange challenge, you tell the last joke. "Tell me, why is a Dralasite big, wrinkled, and gray?"

The guard looks stunned. It hadn't expected a Dralasite joke from a human kid.

Expecting a really dumb answer, it says, "Okay, kid, but this better be good. Why is a Dralasite big, wrinkled, and gray?"

"Because if it were small, smooth, and white, you might mistake it for an aspirin."

Your last weapon fired, you sit back, heart pounding, to wait for the verdict. You feel Jac's hand on your shoulder.

There's no sound from the guard. Suddenly the needler rifle seems to jump from its lap. Its body puffs into a round ball that begins to roll around the grass. From the middle of the rolling ball comes a strange, high-pitched roar of laughter.

As you watch the ball roll around, you hear amid the laughter, ". . . you might mistake it for an aspirin!"

"Okay, kid," says the human guard. "I guess that means you can get out of here. I'll just turn my back and you skedaddle on out of this camp just as quick as you can. And be sure no one sees you!"

You're out and free! You can't believe it. Whoever would have thought your sister's silly jokes would have some value!

The other pirates are working over by the

storehouse. No one sees you and Jac making your way to the time machine.

But you have to hurry. There's no telling how long the guards will keep their promise.

You notice as you run that there seem to be very few footprints near the crystalline structure. The pirates must not have figured out what it is. That's good.

With Pongo at your heels, you and Jac crouch behind the big crystalline structure, hidden from the pirates.

"Okay," you say, catching your breath, "now that we're here, what do we do?"

"I was thinking while you were asking the Dralasite those awful riddles—for which we must remember to thank your sister!—and came up with two alternatives, both involving this wonderful machine.

1) "We could go to an earlier time and do something that would prevent the pirates from establishing a camp here." Turn to page 78.

2) "Or we could try to reach the time just between when that cargo ship landed and the pirates reached it. Maybe we could get the crew to take us home." Turn to page 68.

You turn toward the rocks and trees, certain that you'll find help. You have walked only a few minutes when you see a flash of silver ahead. Just as you step onto a rock, you hear a sound that makes you stop abruptly.

"Ting! That was a shout! A human shout!"

You hurry around a large outcropping of rock and see that, yes, indeed — you did hear a human voice. There, ahead of you, are a human and two Yazirians. They are working with surveying equipment.

You approach the human, who appears to be the leader of the group. "Please, sir, I'm lost and need to get home."

"What's this? What's this? A youngster! How did you get here?" the human asks.

You tell your story. Happily you learn that the surveyors work for your father's company and are in regular radio contact.

Within only a few hours, your father sends a spaceship for you and you are on your way home. Your only souvenir of the adventure is a green feather.

THE END

"Let's go to the cargo ship, Jac. That seems more useful if we're trying to get home," you say.

"But what about the pirates, Kyiki?" asks Jac. "They were still in camp when we saw the ship. We mustn't let them see us!"

Thinking hard, you say, "They were getting ready to leave the camp. And remember—we know the pirates went the long way from the camp, so the crew could unload the ship. Maybe I can get us to where we'd have enough time to reach the ship before the pirates get there."

"All right. If you really think so," says Jac with doubt in his voice.

You grasp the knob and turn it very, very gently. When the knob clicks into place, a low roar fills your ears. You look up and see the cargo ship just coming into sight. Looking toward the camp, you see the pirates beginning to get excited. And you hear a shout: "Time for action, boys!"

"Perfect timing!" you say to Jac. "Let's go!"

Stepping off the platform on the side away from the camp, you hear a whine behind you. It's Pongo, looking very sad, as if he realizes that you're leaving.

You rub his head and think wishfully about taking the strange green winged creature home with you. But then you say, "I'm sorry, Pongo. You belong here."

You stand, try to get a stern look on your face, and say, "Stay here, Pongo!" The animal whimpers a bit but stays on the platform as you turn to leave.

You and Jac run through the trees until you can see the cargo ship landing. As you watch, a large door opens in the ship's side.

"Wait!" Jac stops abruptly, and you stumble across a couple of his legs.

As you pick yourself up, Jac says, "Sorry, Kyiki. But I think we'd better give some more thought to what we're doing. We don't know who's on that ship. Let's just think for a minute.

1) "Shall we just go up to the ship and try to persuade the crew, whoever they may be, to let us on board?" If so, turn to page 136.

2) "Or shall we be cautious and watch for a few minutes? Maybe we can get some idea of whom the ship belongs to." If that is your choice, turn to page 116.

Beginning to get the knack of riding the loper, you relax and stretch your arms.

You realize that you're still carrying Ting. Happily you turn on the Compu-Pal and enjoy the fact that it never doubts your word. It just accepts the fact that you're riding on a dinosaur on a strange planet. You describe where you are heading.

"So I thought I might get help at the village on the hillside," you end.

"Seems reasonable, Kyiki. What are you seeing now?" Ting asks.

"Well . . ." You look around. For the first time you realize you're not alone. "We're riding past fields being cultivated by strange creatures. They have large jointed, spidery legs, and three-lobed bodies. Oh, and they have three eyes!" Then you whisper, "They must see us, but they don't react."

Soon you see that you are indeed headed toward a village. More of the creatures are coming out of their houses on the rocky hillsides and are looking toward you.

"Maybe you should approach them on foot, Kyiki," suggests Ting.

"Yes," you agree, and you stop the loper.

"Thanks, boy," you say to the animal, and then you climb down its back.

Perhaps twenty of the creatures gather on a hillside and walk toward you in a V-shaped line. At the head of the V marches a creature wearing a scarf of red, purple, and white wrapped around its upper body.

The V parts, and the creatures march around you in a distinct dancing rhythm. They don't seem threatening.

The scarfed creature stops before you. It makes strange noises, as if it expects you to understand. You look puzzled, and it changes the sounds it makes. When you still look puzzled, it changes the sounds again.

Then you hear, "Edestekai welcome you."

"Thank you," you say, relieved that these creatures can speak your language.

"Come," the scarfed leader tells you. It turns and signals you to follow. You come to a three-sided pyramid made of beautiful columns of crystal and rock.

"This is our temple. I am the priest," explains the leader. "Sit." The priest points to a seat covered with a red, purple, and white cloth. "Tell us who you are."

You tell them everything that has happened since the crash. Then you ask if they can contact your father.

"We have radio, left by beings who tried to steal our lands. How do Edestekai know that you, too, will not to try to harm us?"

"The only thing I want is to get home," you say.

"We must be sure you are telling the truth," the leader says. "We have a way to be certain. You will submit to the quickdeath test. If you survive, we know you are telling the truth. If you choose not to submit to the test, we cannot believe you. We must protect ourselves."

"Quick death!" you exclaim, frightened. "How can I survive a quick death?"

"A quickdeath is a creature of justice," the priest says. "Only the innocent can survive. Come, I will show you."

Reluctantly, you follow the priest to a dark corner. There in a cage is a large creature covered with skin of shiny armor. Four eyes grow on stalks above the fang-toothed mouth. Long catlike legs end in curved, sharp claws. Out of the creature's sides grow writhing tentacles. Its long tail has a nasty-looking barb at the end.

The entire animal seems to be made for death and destruction. Yours!

"Is fighting this . . . THING! . . . the only way I can get you to help me?" you whisper in horror.

"Yes. We cannot radio strangers to come without being absolutely certain that they will not try to destroy us. However," the priest adds, "the choice is yours."

1) "Don't do it, Kyiki!" says Ting. "I can't see the creature, but it sounds terrible. Don't take chances." If this is your choice, turn to page 35.

2) "But surely I should do whatever I can to get home," you reply. If you agree, turn to page 124.

"Since we know we can get back to today, let's try the time machine again," you say.

Jac hesitates. "Okay, Kyiki. But I insist that we change time only in small amounts. We just don't know enough Volturnian history to take a chance."

"Okay. I'll just turn it a tiny bit."

You, Jac, and Pongo gather around the control knob. Pongo grabs at the crystals.

"Stop it, Pongo! Bad boy!" you shout.

You turn back to the time machine, take hold of the knob, and turn it slightly.

There is a blinding flash. When it clears, you see that the scene around you has changed only slightly.

"Duck, Kyiki!" whispers Jac urgently.

You duck without questioning why. Then, peeking around the pedestal, you see why. The camp is alive with monkeylike Yazirians, insect-shaped Vrusk, humans, even a couple of Dralasites.

"What do you suppose these people are doing here?" you ask.

"I don't know," says Jac, puzzled.

"Maybe they can help us." Just as you're about to show yourself, you hear a shout. You see a large Yazirian, dressed in black, cracking a big whip. The whip descends on the long back of a Vrusk. Jac winces in sympathy.

"Next time, maybe you'll remember your orders!" barks the big Yazirian.

"We'd better get back to our own time," you whisper. Jac nods in agreement.

You reach for the knob, but Jac stops you. "Wait!" he says. "Look over there."

You look where he is pointing and see a large spaceship descending. As you watch, the ship disappears behind some trees. The people in the camp are busy gathering weapons excitedly. The Yazirian in black shouts, "Take the long way around. Let them do all the work before we take their cargo!"

"They're going to hijack that ship!" you gasp. "Let's get out of here, quick!"

"Right!" agrees Jac. "But be careful."

Slowly you reach for the knob and turn it ever so slightly back. The sky fills with a golden light as it clicks gently into place.

"Okay," Jac breathes with relief. "We're gone. They're gone. At least we're safe."

"Hey, Jac! Look! The camp is just like they left it. We moved only an hour or so!"

"Right! That means they could be back at any time. We have two choices, Kyiki:

1) "If we go back to the time we were just in, maybe we can reach the cargo ship before the pirates. We might both escape and save the cargo, too." If this is your choice, turn to page 68.

2) "Or let's go back farther in time and see if we can find another way to get home." If this is your choice, turn to page 45.

You look again to your right and murmur, "I bet they won't want me to bring Ting."

"Think twice, Kyiki," Ting cautions.

"Ting, I can't leave you behind!"

You open the hatch and see a small round pod that is a tiny spaceship. Its clear top is off. There is just enough room for you and Ting. A large sign before you says simply:

PRESS BUTTON TO ACTIVATE.
PSP WILL EJECT AUTOMATICALLY
WHEN G FORCE/HEAT REACHES
PRESET LEVEL.

"What about Jac, Kyiki?" Ting asks. Then the loudspeaker crackles, "Evacuate now."

"We've got to go, Ting!" You pull the top down, breathe deeply, and press the button.

Nothing happens for a minute. Then you hear a low hum. A needle on a dial rises slowly toward a green light.

"Should I do something?" you start to ask Ting, but an unseen force pushes you down into the seat. Looking up, you see that your PSP is arcing away from the spaceship.

You relax, momentarily weightless until gravity begins to pull the PSP toward Volturnus. The g force binds you to the seat again until . . . THUD! You've landed.

The humming stops, but dials begin to move. They show an atmospheric reading in the "SAFE" range and a temperature of 27 degrees C. under a slightly greenish sky.

The plastic hood pops open. You look up but see no sign of your spaceship. You don't know if it crashed or not.

You panic as you check the antenna of the automatic beacon. It's gone! What if no signal is broadcasting? No one will know where you are—alone on a strange planet!

"What are you seeing, Kyiki?" Ting's raspy voice startles you. Sometimes his questions annoy you, but you're glad your father gave you the Compu-Pal. Ting helps you with your studies, discusses decisions with you, and, in fact, is your friend.

"We're on a flat plain, with a few trees nearby. Off in the distance are some hills, and I think I see a dust cloud. . . . Hey! It looks like a herd of big animals."

"Remember, Kyiki," Ting reminds you, "there is intelligent life on Volturnus."

"Yeah, that's right. Maybe there's somebody here who can help us," you say.

What do you want to do?

1) Stay with the PSP, hoping that the automatic beacon will summon help. Turn to page 105.

2) Set a signal fire to try to attract attention. Turn to page 27.

3) Head for the herd of animals and try to find help. Turn to page 138.

"Jac!" you suddenly exclaim in horror. "I don't remember whether I turned the knob to the right or the left before!"

"Stay calm, Kyiki. Close your eyes and try to remember," suggests Jac.

You close your eyes and try to make the muscles in your hand and arm remember. "I don't know, Jac!" you say in despair. "Maybe I better test it just a little."

Just as you close your eyes, you notice Pongo bounce off into the woods. You turn the knob just a tiny bit to the right. Then you open your eyes and take a quick look around.

"Jac! Look!" you exclaim. The trees around you are blackened and bare. The camp is gone and in its place is scattered rubble.

"There must have been—no, there's going to be—a huge fire," you say. "Well, I'll turn it the other way."

When you look, the pirate camp is gone once again. But this time it has never been there. The trees are young and fresh, perhaps a little older than when you saw them the first time you used the machine. And this time Jac doesn't disappear, because he is standing on the platform next to you.

"It looks like the proper time, but what are we going to do to make sure the pirates don't build a camp here?" you ask.

"Not a fire. This is too dry a planet. We might not be able to control it."

"Well, if not fire, how about water? Look. The land forms a shallow basin where the pirates built their camp. We could use that stream to flood the basin. Then the pirates can't be here when our ship crashes."

"Good thinking, student!" Jac looks at you approvingly. "But then there's the next question—how do we divert the stream?"

"Do we dare go back to our time for a moment?" you ask. "Maybe the pirates have some explosives we could bring back."

"Seems reasonable. But let me go for the explosives, Kyiki. There are Vrusk in camp, so I'm probably safer than you."

"Okay," you say reluctantly.

Again you turn the knob. You're sure you'll find the pirates standing right by the time machine, but, no, this time you're safe. Instead, Pongo greets you like a long-lost friend.

"Quiet, Pongo! They mustn't know we're here!" you whisper as Jac darts off.

With Pongo in your arms, you crouch behind the crystal structure of the time machine. The wait seems endless.

All at once, Jac is running as fast as he can toward you, his arms full. Several pirates are chasing him.

"Get ready to change time!" Jac shouts.

You position yourself by the pedestal. You can't turn the knob until Jac reaches you, but the pirates are right behind him.

Then Jac leaps, eight-legged, onto the platform. A pirate jumps, too, but Jac kicks him off. You turn the knob and see a look of amazement on the pirate's face as . . .

ROSLOF

You check the trees and make a tiny adjustment of the knob. You breathe a sigh of relief—you're back in the time where you want to be!

"Thanks," Jac gasps. "That was good timing."

While Jac catches his breath, you look at what he found in the pirate camp—two boxes of plastic explosives, a small box of detonators, and food!

Hungrily, you gobble the chewy meat mixture. Once Jac satisfies his hunger, he takes small chunks of plastic explosives and places a detonator in each.

You search for a good, strong stick and a rock. Using the rock as a hammer, you tap the stick into the ground and then pull it out again. You make holes evenly spaced from the stream to the basin, far enough from the time machine to be safe. Jac follows you, dropping explosives, detonator, and a tiny timer into each hole.

Carrying Pongo, you quickly return with Jac to the platform. As you reach it, the first explosion goes off, then another.

"Three . . . four . . . five." Jac counts until all the charges have gone off.

By the time you reach the trench, water floods the opening, headed for the basin.

"Volturnus has a new lake!" you exclaim.

"I just hope it stops the pirates from making a camp here. All we can do is go back to our own time and find out," says Jac.

"Okay. Everybody on board?" you sing out, feeling like the captain of a ship.

"Better stop talking, Kyiki. If this hasn't worked, there's no need to call attention to ourselves," your tutor cautions you.

Quietly, you turn the knob. Again you hold your breath, as if that might have some effect on what happens.

There's no sign of the pirates. The trees are larger again. Strange wild flowers grow along the edge of a small, clear lake.

"I name you Lake Kyiki," you proclaim, tossing a flower into the water.

"We're safe now," says Jac, "but we'd better think about what to do next."

"Maybe we'd better split up," you suggest. "The chances of our finding help might double."

"Kyiki, your father entrusted your safety to me. Besides, if one of us got help, how would we let the other one know?"

You hold out your wrist, which bears a chronocom, the combination radio and calculator.

"Right," says Jac, glancing at his own chronocom. "We can choose."

1) If you choose to go off on your own for turn to page 37.

2) If you want to stay with Jac and see what happens, turn to page 15.

"Yes. I'm sure they'll help me," you think.

You put your shoes back on and start toward the voices.

Suddenly you realize that Arnla is holding back. As you look back at her, she says, "I'm not coming, Kyiki."

"Not coming! Why?"

"You'll get help from the humans and go home. I have to return to my clutch. They will be angry that I left the herd to go with you. Good-bye, Kyiki. I'll miss you." And Arnla turns and hurries back through the passages, but not before you notice the tears in her eyes.

Sadly you watch until she disappears. Then you hear the voices again. You feel sure they must be surveyors, working for your father. What luck!

You walk boldly around the corner and see two humans and two of the monkeylike Kurabanda.

"Hello," you say simply.

"What? Who are you?" demands one of the humans.

"My name is Kyiki. My spaceship crashed on Volturnus and I need to get home to my father."

"So who's your father, kid?" asks the first human.

"The head of Universal Minerals, the company you're working for."

"How do you know that, kid?" asks one of the monkeylike creatures suspiciously.

"Their symbol is on your hat."

"I hate to tell you this, kid, but you're fresh out of luck. We aren't working for Universal—not anymore. We're selling the information to the Sathar, who intend to use it to help them control this planet."

Your relief changes to fear.

The other human speaks for the first time. "Let's just hold on to this kid awhile and see who wants to pay the most, the father or the Sathar."

You turn to run but find the Kurabanda have moved behind you and are pointing pistols at you.

It's clear that these people aren't going to help you. You're in big trouble!

THE END

"Good-bye, Arnla," you say. "Thank you for wanting to help. But I think I had better go on by myself."

The Ul-Mor girl looks sad for a moment, then takes a green feather from her headdress and gives it to you. Her mind-link tentacle creeps onto your neck again.

"Do you have something you can give me? I'll tell the others I stole it."

"What? Why would you tell them you stole it?" you ask, not understanding.

"The tribe will think I'm clever if I steal from a stranger. Maybe the elders will let me herd the kwidges more often," says Arnla.

You think of the different things you have in your pouches. Nothing seems right until you remember the electronic chess set you always carry with you. You dig it out of your pocket and proudly show it to her.

Arnla looks at the screen and buttons, and her face falls in disappointment. Then you turn the set on and the board lights up, showing the chessmen where you left them after playing with Ting during your flight. As you press buttons and the men move around, Arnla's face grows excited.

You hand Arnla the set and she says, a little shyly, "I won't say I stole this. I'll keep it for myself. Kyiki, I hope you get to your family safely."

Please turn to page 12.

"Kyiki?" the radio crackles again. "Is that you? Where are you?"

"Just read the paper, kid," Gorlo says.

"It's me, Dad." You pause a moment and look at the Dralasite. "Dad, I'm all right. But would you please turn off the computer in my room. I was studying before I—"

A hand slaps over your mouth. "No chat, kid," Gorlo says gruffly.

The hand loosens and you mumble, "I just don't want my computer to burn out. I'll read the message."

The Dralasite removes its gray hand from your mouth. You must try not to show your relief at having told your dad about the computer. You hadn't really left it on, but he'll probably go read what you were working on before you left. You were studying what was known about the Eorna civilization on Volturnus!

You read the paper, which tells the kidnappers' demands and how your father should meet them. The moment you finish reading, the engineer grabs the paper and yanks your personal crystal from the radio.

You are hustled back to your room and left there. You are anxious because you don't know if your dad will yield or not.

For a couple of days, the guards keep a closer eye on you, but gradually you are free to wander again. You decide to look for that important holodisc. You don't know what it is, but maybe it will help.

You try to avoid running into guards as you explore. A couple of times you overhear guards mention that there has been no word from your father. You're glad that your father hasn't given in to their demands, but you feel a bit forlorn and unloved.

One day you notice a door you've never noticed before. You open the door and discover a storage room of some sort. Mounted on one wall are numerous weapons, some of them strange and unusual. Another wall bears shelves of ammunition and medical equipment. On a third wall are various cabinets.

You peer out into the corridor to make sure no one is coming. Propping the door open slightly so that you can hear anyone approaching, you begin to explore the cabinets. The first contains clothing. The second holds small parts used in repairing robots. The third contains holobelts and holodiscs.

You read the labels quickly. They say such things as "Scenery for Invisibility" and "Young Yazirian." You even see one labeled "Jac," which the Dralasite must have used when it kidnapped you. You see nothing of special interest and start to turn away when you realize that you almost missed a small drawer. You pull at it, but it doesn't open. It must have some special kind of lock.

You inspect the drawer closely. There is no sign of a lock or a latch.

You are holding onto the edges of the drawer, thinking about possibilities. Suddenly you hear a click and the front panel folds downward, opening the small locked section. It must be a thermal lock. You wouldn't have discovered that if you hadn't held onto the drawer long enough to warm it.

You reach in and pull out a holodisc. It has no label, just a number—1707.

It must be important, you think, or it wouldn't be in a specially locked drawer. You decide to take it with you, on the chance that it might be useful.

After checking the corridor to see if anyone is near, you tuck a holobelt and the unlabeled disc in your belt pouch. You leave the room and quickly shut the door behind you. Ducking low, you scoot down the corridor, hoping you won't be noticed.

Once in your own room, you put on the holobelt and insert the disc. You hold your breath as you flick the switch on the belt.

You look down at yourself. Blast! Nothing is changed. Now, why should that be? The belt appears to be functioning all right. The disc is inserted properly. The power unit is on. So why doesn't anything happen?

You look around for a mirror, hoping that maybe the disc is working but you can't see its image because you're behind it. Then you remember that there is no mirror in your room. You always have to go to the hygiene room down the hall in the morning.

You decide to risk it. You open the door quietly and peek out. You neither see nor hear

anything, so you start down the hall to the left. As you turn the corner, two guards round the corner ahead, coming toward you.

Certain you've been seen, you hurry back to your room. You listen anxiously as they pass.

"That was the Boss, wasn't it?" one says. "I thought he had an appointment with the Sathar." The steps disappear down the corridor.

The Boss! You must have on a holodisc of the Boss! You were right about that mystery disc. You feel like you, but you must look like him. How strange!

You've got an advantage now—or do you? They think you are the Boss, the man they take orders from. You ponder how best to use your new disguise.

You decide you have three choices:

1) You mostly want to get out of here, so you choose to wear the holodisc to try to escape. Turn to page 130.

2) There's no point in escaping unless you can get off the planet, so you use the holodisc to try to get to the radio room to call your father. Turn to page 42.

3) Because some guards know the Boss is away, you decide it would be too dangerous to use. Turn to page 48.

"There's no telling who or what might be on the other side of that guard. I think we should go back up into the desert. At least there we can see what's coming."

You and Arnla tiptoe back the way you came and climb out into the sunlight.

"Whew! I sure like daylight better than dark caves," you say. But no answer comes from Arnla, just a wave of sadness.

"What's the matter, Arnla?"

"I think I must go back to my herd, Kyiki. Quin-Quin will have returned without me, and my tribe will be worried, maybe even angry, since I'm not with the herd."

"Would it help if I gave you something that you can say you stole?" you ask.

"Oh, yes, please, Kyiki!"

You explore your pouch and find the miniature electronic chess set.

"Here, Arnla. This is a game called chess." You turn it on, and Arnla's face lights up as the set does. She takes it and joyfully presses buttons, watching the chessmen move around the checkered screen.

"I won't give this to the tribe. I'll keep it for myself. Thank you, Kyiki. I must go now."

Arnla disconnects her mind-link but hugs you fondly with two other tentacles. You still feel her friendship toward you as she waves good-bye and walks away.

Please turn to page 12.

You think for a moment and suddenly feel very tired. There really has been enough excitement for one day.

"You're right, Jac. I'd really like to get home now."

You and Jac split up to explore each of the huts in the camp. In one of them, you find a powerful radio.

You remove from the chain around your neck your personal radio crystal. It fits into any radio and automatically calls your father's private frequency.

Fumbling in your eagerness, you place the crystal in the radio. Within a minute, you hear the rumble of your father's voice.

"Hello. Kyiki? Is that you?"

"Yes, Father. Jac and I are on Volturnus and need your help." Quickly you explain your predicament.

"I'm glad you're not hurt, Kyiki. Now, go back to the PSP, and I'll divert the nearest shuttle to pick you up. Then we'll have troops take care of those pirates."

With relief, you sign off and pull your crystal from the radio.

When you leave the hut, you see no one from the cargo ship. But then you notice one member, a Yazirian, in a tree. The crew must have an ambush prepared for the pirates.

Standing under the tree, you call, "I've radioed my father. We're to go back to the rescue pod and wait for a shuttle he's sending. He's sending troops, too."

The Yazirian calls down, "You and Jac go ahead to the shuttle, kid. We've got a personal score to settle with those thugs. And we've got to look after our captain." Then it adds, "Be sure your father hurries those troops. We need all the help we can get."

Pongo, who has been following you around the camp, is still at your heels. You bend down and say, "Oh, Pongo. What am I going to do with you?" He flops on his back so you can rub his tummy.

"Mom wouldn't let me have a space-cat, but she never said anything about a furry green flying frog, or whatever you are. Come on, fella. You're going home with me."

"Come on, Kyiki. We have to get out of here before the pirates return," Jac urges.

With Pongo riding on Jac's long back, you set off quickly toward the PSP. Just as it comes into sight, you hear the sound of rifle fire from the camp. The pirates must have returned. You hope the ship's crew took them completely by surprise.

But even if the pirates won this time, they won't the next time. You know your father will send troops to stop the pirates, and Volturnus will again be safe for exploration.

THE END

You feel you'll die unless you get water. You know water has special value here. Maybe if you paid for it, it would be okay.

You creep to the roofed structure in the middle of the village. Eagerly you draw the bucket up from the well and drink thirstily.

After drinking your fill, you pull a Uni-pen from your pouch and search for a bit of paper. You quickly write a note:

THANK YOU FOR THE WATER.
I AM LEAVING 5CR TO PAY FOR IT.
KYIKI

You leave the note and some PermaPlastik credit coins on the well and scurry back to the mound. You quickly drop back to sleep.

"THIEF!"

The harsh cry wakens you. Arnla's mother stands by your couch, her ninth tentacle on your spine. Arnla is at the foot of the couch, looking worried. Four Ul-Mor elders crowd behind Kon-Dudro. They keep sending angry glances your way.

You know that paying for the water was not enough. "I'm sorry," you say to Arnla.

She looks too frightened to reply. But there is understanding in her eyes.

You look back to Kon-Dudro to explain. "I was so thirsty . . . and I paid for it."

"The pay doesn't matter," she says sadly. "The water belongs to the One Who is Many. The council must decide what to do with you."

The Ul-Mor with the most elaborate head-dress makes a sign to Kon-Dudro.

You feel both dismay and relief coming from her mind as she glances worriedly at Arnla. Then she says to you, "The council has decided to banish you to the desert." She removes her tentacle from your spine, and you feel as if all caring has also been removed.

Arnla reaches over and says, "I'm sorry."

"Yeah. Me, too, Arnla. I was just so-o-o-o thirsty. Thanks for trying to help me."

The Ul-Mor elders surround you and begin to push you out of the mound, giving you only a second to grab Ting. One elder mounts a huge loper and the others place you in front of him. Instantly the loper starts to move.

When the Ul-Mor halts the loper, you are far from the village, in barren desert. The Ul-Mor drops you to the black, parched ground. The loper turns at his signal and gallops off toward the Ul-Mor village.

You are alone. Again.

You are no nearer getting off Volturnus than you were yesterday. What do you do now?

1) If you choose to sneak back to the village, find Arnla, and try to get her help, turn to page 16.

2) If you want to go back to your Personal Safety Pod, turn to page 123.

You don't know what's happening, or why. But you don't want to be kidnapped! You prepare to leap, hoping to avoid injury.

Off in the distance, to your left, you see what might be a forested area, with lots of rocks among the trees. That's where you'll head!

The Dralasite's attention is on driving the hovercycle, so you slowly reach out and grab Ting's handle. Then you brace your foot and prepare to leap.

As the hovercycle enters a clear area free from rocks, you see your chance. Relaxing your body to help avoid breaking anything, you roll cleanly and get up running.

Behind you, you hear the sound you were hoping for—the metallic thud of the hovercycle crashing. You must have startled the Dralasite enough for it to lose control.

You know that if you run hard, the Dralasite will never be able to catch up. Even when Dralasites grow extra legs, they can't run as fast as humans. So you stand a good chance of getting away.

You run without looking back and with a power born of the need to survive. Soon you can run no longer. Your legs give way beneath you, and you fall in the grass, panting for breath. You rest for only a moment—you've got to get out of sight.

Taking a moment to look back, you see in the distance the dark, lumpish figure of the Dralasite. It seems to be bending over the hovercycle, kicking the machine.

Chuckling with satisfaction, you make your way into the cool dimness of the woods.

Feeling pretty safe now, you click on Ting, your Compu-Pal.

"Hi, Ting. Lots has been happening."

"Tell me about it, Kyiki. I can guess from the way I'm being jostled that we're walking. But the last I knew, we were on the laboratory ship."

You tell Ting about the ship crashing and being kidnapped by the strange Dralasite.

"Come now, Kyiki. I thought you outgrew making up fantastic tales a long time ago."

"No, Ting! It's all true!"

You start to describe to him where you are and realize that you have left the protection of the woods.

Your eyes blink from the glare of the sun as you step out from beneath the trees. You have to squint to look into the distance.

Your eyes widen as you see a billow of dust far off. You watch a little longer and you see what might be large animals raising the dust.

"Ting! I think I see big animals over there. If it's a herd, maybe there's someone herding them."

"Or maybe there's more danger, Kyiki. Think twice."

Please turn to page 39.

"If we just try to trick the guard, it might come back and catch us while we're broadcasting. I think we'd better make sure it can't, at least for a while."

You pull a copper-colored tube from your pouch. "All I have to do is touch the guard with this and, zoom, we head for the radio."

"Okay, Kyiki. I will follow you." Then Arnla looks at you strangely and says, "Good luck!" as if she doubts you will have it.

You creep toward the radio room. You feel Arnla disconnect the mind-link, not wanting to distract you.

You stop outside the radio room and set the knob on the copper tube to "STUN." Taking a deep breath and holding the Stunstick ready, you dive into the room.

Instead of one unsuspecting guard on a noisy chair, there are three large Kurabanda pointing laser pistols right at you.

"Hey, it's a human kid . . . and one of those purple octopuses." The largest Kurabanda, the leader, laughs. "No wonder the trembler alarms went crazy. It thought there was a whole gang coming."

A suspicious look crosses its face and it looks out into the corridor. "Nope, there aren't any more out here," it says in relief, and on its face suspicion changes to evil.

You're trapped. You should have known that one chair scrape and one cough didn't mean there was just one person in here. You try to hide your Stunstick back of your leg.

But then you see the radio behind a guard. Maybe you can reach it after all.

Suddenly you swing your Stunstick up, ready to jab out at the guards. You thrust toward one and watch it fall back, surprised. You quickly turn toward the second one, but before you can touch it, the third guard—the one who laughed—grabs your arm. The Stunstick spins across the room, and your arm is yanked around and up your back.

"Who are you?" demands the Kurabanda.

"My spaceship crashed. I'm just—" you gasp in pain—"just trying to get home."

"Well, home's not down here, kid. Why were you spying on us?" the guard demands.

"I am Kyiki. My father is head of Universal Minerals."

"Universal!" exclaims one guard. "Do you suppose they already know?"

"It doesn't matter," says the leader. "We'll be out of here right away. And since Universal won't be paying for our information, we'll just let them pay to get the kid back. The purple octopus can stay here until we clear out."

You know that you can't do any more right now. You'll just have to wait until your father pays the ransom the crooks will demand. Or will you? Maybe the guards will get careless and you'll be able to get away. You're certainly not just going to give up.

THE END

You are certain Jac will be at the main rescue capsule with the rest of the group.

You go down the aisle toward the others. But when you look into the capsule, you don't see your tutor. It shouldn't be that difficult to see Jac—after all, Vrusk have eight legs on their segmented bodies and take up a lot of room!

"Hey, Kyiki!" you hear a voice say. It's Jac, at another pod on your left.

"There's room in here for both of us, Kyiki."

Because this Personal Safety Pod is specially made to hold a large Vrusk, there is room for you to squeeze in with Jac, who is rather slender for a Vrusk. He crosses two of his legs over the others, leaving room for you to climb in and strap yourself in.

Jac pulls the clear top over your heads, bolting it tight. In front of your eyes is a sign:

PRESS BUTTON TO ACTIVATE.
PSP WILL EJECT AUTOMATICALLY
WHEN G FORCE/HEAT REACHES
PRESET LEVEL.

You press the button. At first nothing happens. Then you realize that a light has begun to glow on the instrument panel. It's white, then yellow, then green. A counter starts to flick: 1 . . . 2 . . . 3. But nothing more happens. You press the button again, thinking you've done something wrong.

Then suddenly you are forced back into

your couch. Straining to raise your head to look through the plastic, you see that your pod has rocketed away from the main craft. As you watch, struggling to hold up your head against the g force, the rocket engine shuts off.

You enjoy a few moments of weightlessness. Then once again the g forces push you down into the couch. The descent rockets land your PSP with a thud on Volturnus's soil.

"Aerodynamic landing is more comfortable than descent rockets, but at least we are down safely," Jac says as he unfastens the straps that hold his long body in place.

"Is it safe to open the top?" you wonder. Then you notice that several dials on the instrument panel are still moving. The atmosphere reading settles into the "SAFE" zone and the temperature gauge stops at 27 degrees C. It's a pleasant day under a slightly greenish sky.

You and Jac slide the clear top back and look around.

You neither see nor hear anything of the main ship . . . or of anything else.

"Are we alone?" you ask in a whisper.

"Looks that way, Kyiki," Jac answers.

"How are we going to get home?"

"Presumably, the captain radioed that the ship was going down. Hmmm. Too bad there's no radio in this pod. We'll set the automatic beacon and hope someone picks up the signal."

"Do we have to stay right here?" you ask.

"Well," says Jac thoughtfully, "it certainly would be safer if rescue is on the way. However, I thought I saw some smoke over there in those foothills to our left and also in those woods over there.

"What do you think we should do, Kyiki? And please explain your reasoning. These are our choices:

1) "First and foremost—stay right here by the pod. Let's not take any chances on being missed." If this is your choice, turn to page 13.

2) "There is a collapsible hovercycle under the couch in the pod. We could leave a note on the pod and go for a short ride." If you want to use the hovercycle, turn to page 119.

3) "Perhaps we ought to explore nearby, in the vicinity of the PSP." If this is your choice, turn to page 25.

"We're going to stay here, Ting," you say firmly. "Maybe the beacon works without its antenna and someone has already received our signal. If they come looking, they'll expect to find us right here."

"You sound very certain, Kyiki," says Ting.

"I am! I'm also hungry!"

You look over the side of the PSP into the cushioned seat. You notice a latch you hadn't seen before. When you turn the latch, a tiny door opens, revealing a canteen of water and small packets of dried food. At least you won't be hungry or thirsty.

Sitting down in the shade of your PSP, you say, "Let's play chess, Ting."

You are content to wait quietly until help comes. You are certain that a message will have gone out from the spaceship to your home planet telling them of your trouble. And you think that your beacon may be working even without an antenna. So you are sure that someone will be there soon.

By nightfall, you are not so certain. You spend the night curled up in the PSP, feeling cold and lonely. When morning comes, Ting, still sounding cheerful, says, "Maybe you'd better reconsider your decision, Kyiki."

Please go back to page 77
and make another choice.

-ROSLOF

"Your people would be upset if the desert were destroyed, wouldn't they?" you ask.

"Of course! We need to be able to herd kwidges in the desert to live."

"Do you think your people would help us stop these guys from stealing the Volturnian minerals and destroying the desert?"

"Oh, yes. Let's go talk to them."

You go back through the caves the way you came, stopping only to put your shoes on. There is no sign of the Kurabanda guard as you tiptoe past the side corridor.

Coming out into the sunlight, you hear a loud snuffling sound. There stands Quin-Quin, Arnla's loper. What luck! Now you can ride quickly to the Ul-Mor village and get the help you need. The Ul-Mor should help to prevent the surveyors from selling the secrets of Volturnus to the Sathar. Then you'll be able to radio your father and be rescued and help him at the same time.

Rescue in sight at last, you and Arnla climb on the loper's back and ride toward the Ul-Mor village.

THE END

At first you see only rock, jumbled in great mounds. Then, as you look more closely, you begin to realize that the rocks are actually the roofs of structures of some sort.

Gradually, you recognize beautiful, complex patterns in the rock structures—not a jumble at all.

Then you feel the zapgun in your back.

"Move!" demands the Dralasite.

"Where?" you ask.

"Over to that black carved door." The Dralasite gestures toward a door you hadn't noticed. The door opens and you see a monkeylike figure frowning at you and the Dralasite. It holds a rifle in its arms.

"What took so long, you lump?" asks the monkey angrily. "The Boss is waiting."

"We're here now, so keep your Kurabanda cackle to yourself."

The Dralasite and the Kurabanda are obviously not friends, you decide.

You are led into a huge, ornate room. The walls are carved and painted in reds, greens, blues, yellows. Set into the walls are beautiful small sculptures, some of natural crystals, others clearly created by patient, loving hands.

The Kurabanda and the Dralasite push you down a corridor and through a door. A human and a Vrusk sit at a table. You wonder about Jac as you see the Vrusk.

"Are we supposed to take the kid straight to the Boss?" the Dralasite behind you asks.

"Nope," drawls the human. "All he wants to

-ROSLOF

know is that Kyiki is here. There's a room waiting down the hall. Take Kyiki there now, Gorlo."

Well, at least they're not in any hurry to harm you, you think as the Dralasite leads you away.

You're taken through several beautiful corridors. You pass many doors but don't get any opportunity to look through them. Finally the Dralasite says, "Stop here!"

It presses a plate on the wall and an opening appears. "Okay, kid. Give me that computer you've been carrying—and your chronocom."

"Oh, no!" you exclaim, clutching Ting.

"Hand 'em over, kid."

The Dralasite takes the chronocom as you remove it from your wrist. Then, grabbing Ting from your hand, it pushes you into the room.

That room becomes your prison. You have a bed, a chair, a table, and some microreader discs. You have a lot of time to think about what you want to do.

1) If you decide not to cause any trouble, turn to page 139.

2) If you decide you just can't make things easy for your captors and want to fight back, turn to page 7.

Your mind races as fast as the hovercycle. If you try to jump off, you'll probably be hurt.

You look at the combination radio and calculator on your wrist. The radio reaches only a short distance. How could anyone within its range on this strange planet be anything but an enemy? Using it would probably just bring more trouble down on your head.

You decide to just ride on with this strange Dralasite. For the moment you're safe, and you're likely to get your questions answered.

Trying to relax, you make yourself comfortable for the ride to . . . where?

You realize that the ground is gradually rising. You're heading toward some rocky hillsides. The ground becomes rougher and rougher, making the hovercycle work harder to stay on its cushion of air.

The Dralasite shuts off the engine. As the machine settles to the ground, the Dralasite says gruffly, "Get off. We walk from here." Drawing a small zapgun from its belt, it adds, "Just to make sure you don't try anything silly while we walk."

Please turn to page 108.

Can you really trust a village of novepuses? You wonder a moment, but it's been a long day and you don't want to face the night alone in a strange place.

"Okay, Arnla. I'll go to your village."

"Kyiki! Think twice!" Ting squeaks.

You've heard that too many times, so you impatiently click the computer off.

When you enter the village, you see that the Ul-Mor clutches, or families, live in earthen mounds with round tops. One roofed structure looks like a small shrine.

"Don't be afraid, Kyiki," you feel Arnla say. You're glad to have her with you.

A small flurry of two-legged, hopping animals greets you, yipping excitedly.

"Herd hoppers," Arnla tells you. "They help with the herd."

You look around, fascinated. A large Ul-Mor, his body decorated with many tattoos, rests atop a house mound, sunning himself. He looks angry. You shrink back, but Arnla pulls you along.

"Come on. That's Kon-Krell, my father."

The big novepus places his mind-link tentacle on Arnla. She is still linked to you, so you hear her tell him your story.

Ul-Mor of all sizes gather to inspect you. "They are just curious," Arnla confides. "They have seen humans before, but not right here in our village."

A wrinkled Ul-Mor wearing a small headdress slowly makes her way over to the roofed

-ROSLOF

structure. She lowers a rope and draws it back, bringing up a container.

"Old Rune-Marenga," you feel Arnla say. "She's the Ceremonial Water-Giver."

The old Ul-Mor hobbles back slowly and presents you with a small bowl of water.

"Drink it, Kyiki. It means welcome to our village."

You drink the cool water. As you return the bowl, you feel something at your side. A tentacle has crept quietly into your pocket and removed a small copper tube.

"My vibroknife! Put that back!" you exclaim. The little Ul-Mor runs off, displaying your knife triumphantly. Other little Ul-Mor run over to inspect the prize. The adults just make a sound like laughter.

"Why don't they stop him?" you ask Arnla.

"He's proving that he's growing up."

"By taking MY knife?" you growl.

"He will become important by taking things from people not of our tribe."

"But that's stealing!"

"We like to steal, but never from those of our own village."

"That's wrong!" you grumble to yourself.

Arnla takes you to her clutch's mound. The interior is quite pleasant, with colorful couches and benches around an open fire, where Arnla's mother cooks. Several small Ul-Mor play with tiny clay lopers.

"Good evening, Kon-Dudro Mother. This is my new friend, Kyiki." She pulls you closer.

You bow quickly. "Good evening, Kon-Dudro. Thanks for allowing me in your home."

Arnla's mother wraps you in a big one-tentacle hug and makes you feel welcome.

After a meal of roast kwidge, you are given a couch to rest on while the Ul-Mor tribal council discusses how to help you.

You are tired and fall asleep easily.

You dream of hang gliding on a zero-g planet, over a sun-baked desert. Rising heat waves wrap themselves around you and begin to strangle you.

Suddenly you awaken, your throat parched. It takes a moment to realize where you are.

There was no water supply in the mound—you remember that. But there's a well in the center of the village. You remember Arnla telling you that water is sacred and carefully controlled.

You lie there a few minutes, but soon you can think of nothing but your thirst.

You must make a decision.

1) If you want to go to the well in the center of the village and get a drink, turn to page 95.

2) If you choose to stay in the mound until morning and try to forget your thirst, turn to page 57.

"You're right to be cautious, Jac. Just because the pirates are planning to rob them doesn't mean the ship's crew has to be friendly to us."

"Okay. Let's just stay here and see what we can learn," says Jac.

You settle in the grass behind the trees. You remain alert so that you can run for the ship if it looks as if it might take off.

As you watch, a large Yazirian and two humans start moving boxes down a ramp from the cargo bay to the ground.

Off in the distance, you hear the roar of hovercars. The crew members look puzzled for an instant, then start working again.

In a few minutes, several skimmers roar up to the cargo ship. When they stop, large numbers of Yazirians, Vrusk, humans, and Dralasites pour out and surround the ship.

"It's the guys from the camp!" you whisper. "They weren't supposed to be here yet!"

The newcomers pull out weapons and point them at the crew of the cargo ship.

"We'll just relieve you of that cargo," you hear a voice say.

"No, you don't!" shouts a human from the ship. "This cargo belongs to Universal Minerals!" He struggles to close the bay doors.

But it's too late. A pirate's rifle barks and the man falls.

You watch in horror as the pirates round up the rest of the crew. They force them into one of the hovercars.

As you watch the crew being taken away, you say, "If we hadn't waited, the ship wouldn't have been hijacked. We could have stopped it!"

You think a moment and then add, "Well, at least we can try to help them now. Let's get back to the time machine and see what the pirates do with the crew."

You and Jac make your way back to the big crystalline structure. Pongo appears and dashes joyfully up to you. By the time you have greeted him, you hear a hovercar nearing the camp. It stops and an armed Yazirian and a Dralasite push five prisoners into one of the larger huts. They lock the door, hanging the key from a hook on the frame.

As the Yazirian returns to the car, it shouts to the Dralasite, "You get the truck and we'll get the stuff back here to camp."

Soon both vehicles pull out of the camp, heading toward the cargo ship again.

You and Jac walk over to the hut in which the cargo ship crew is imprisoned.

"Don't worry! We'll get you out," you shout as you unlock the door. At first, the prisoners refuse to come out, thinking that it's some kind of a trick. But after you tell them who you are and how you got there, they come out into the light.

"I suggest we hide until the pirates empty the ship," says Jac.

"No!" exclaims a Yazirian crew member. "We've got to see how the captain is and then try to get the cargo back. We can't let Universal Minerals down. Find some weapons," it says to the other crewmen.

Sticking together in case the pirates come back suddenly, you all search the camp. In one hut you find a store of rifles, pistols, and grenades.

"Kyiki, come here a moment," Jac whispers as the crewmen pick up weapons.

"What's the matter?" you ask when you are out of earshot of the crew.

"I think we'd better leave these people now and make sure we're going to get home. Let's go find the radio," Jac suggests.

"But we can't abandon them," you protest. "There's only five of them, and there's tons of pirates."

1) If you think you should help the ship's crew fight the pirates, turn to page 127.

2) If you want to get to a radio while you can, turn to page 93.

"As long as we leave a note, it should be safe to take a ride. Besides, I really like riding hovercycles."

"Fine! You take care of the note while I get the hovercycle out," says Jac.

You hastily scribble the note and put it in the PSP. Then you join Jac to help him remove the small machine from under the seat.

After drinking some Nutrijuice you find in a small cabinet in the PSP, you check what you have in your belt pouch.

"Okay, Kyiki. Climb on the front seat. I'll use the back. I need room for my legs."

You grab Ting from the PSP and put him in the rack on the hovercycle, determined not to go anywhere without your Compu-Pal friend.

"Do you need to take that talkative thing?" Jac asks.

"Yes, it's my friend!" you say firmly. Then you hop on the front seat and feel the Vrusk's long arms reach around you. One of his feet pushes the starter, and the cycle rises a few inches off the ground and then roars forward on a cushion of air.

"Let's go over that way," you shout above the roar. You point toward some mountains.

You barely hear Jac answer, "I have a better idea." He gives no explanation but heads westward across the open plain. Suddenly the vehicle hits a section of rocks, and the ride becomes bumpy. You look down at the Vrusk's star-shaped hands controlling the hovercycle.

What was that?

-ROSLOF

For just a flash of time, the Vrusk's angular brown arms looked gray and rubbery.

Hmmmm. You must have imagined it, you decide.

You look back up at the changing scenery. The ground gets rougher, and there are more bushes and low trees.

You catch another glimpse of your tutor's arms out of the corner of your eye. Again they look gray and rubbery. You turn in the seat and see a round, blobbish . . . no, there is the shiny, brown face you know so well. Strange.

"Turn around, Kyiki," your tutor says firmly. "Blasted powerpack must be wearing out," he mutters to himself.

"Slow down, Jac," you shout as the ride continues to be quite bumpy.

"Why?" the Vrusk demands.

You turn around and see the truth—he's not Jac! As your eyes widen, the familiar figure of your Vrusk tutor becomes a Dralasite!

For just a second, as you bounce over a rock, the Vrusk flashes back into being. But then the strange Dralasite returns.

"The powerpack on my holobelt must have worn out," the Dralasite says, as if that were some sort of explanation. "I thought there would be enough power to keep my appearance as Jac going through the flight, the crash, and the ride to the complex."

"You knew there was going to be a crash?" you exclaim, bypassing all the other questions that crowd your mind.

"Of course. We arranged it," the strange person says smugly.

"Why?" you ask, not really sure you want to hear the answer.

"We need you, Kyiki. You are a very valuable property to us. We needed to get you here, to where you will be . . . ah, safe."

"But why?" you ask again, angrily.

"Be patient, Kyiki. All will be explained."

You face forward again—angry, puzzled, worried. Why in the universe would a strange Dralasite kidnap you?

You start to think about what you might dare to do.

1) You can jump off the moving hovercycle and try to get away. Turn to page 98

2) You could try to use your chronocom, the communicator on your wrist, in the hope that someone nearby will hear it. Turn to page 134.

3) Or you might just stay quietly on the hovercycle and see where you are taken and try to learn why. Turn to page 111.

You start walking, your back to the sun as it rises in the sky.

Soon your throat begins to get dry again. You remember the lovely coolness of the water you drank during the night. Then you remember that that water is the reason you are here, trudging through the desert heat.

You are beginning to doubt your choice of direction when you see a small group of trees that seem familiar. There, not more than a kilometer to your right, is the silver and green of your PSP, gleaming in the sunlight.

You start to run, pulled by the thought of the shade it makes as well as the idea that perhaps more food and water are stowed in the vehicle.

You find a compartment on the right side that you had not investigated. What luck! It contains an emergency water supply for use in starting the fuel cell. You know it's pure water, and you drink it down in a hurry. Then you relax in the shadow of the pod.

In a few minutes, loneliness overwhelms you. Then you remember Ting! You turn on the Compu-Pal again, and he immediately asks, "What has been happening to us, Kyiki?" You explain, and Ting, good friend that he is, makes no judgments. Instead, you both start to wonder what you can do to let someone know where you are.

Please turn to 27.

The quickdeath has all the advantages, but you want desperately to make these strange Edestekai believe you. If you have to fight some nightmarish fiend, well, you'll just have to do it!

You announce firmly, "I am telling the truth. I will fight that monster."

"So be it." The priest turns to the other Edestekai. "Prepare the quickdeath. There will be a Test of Truthfulness."

You watch as the Edestekai prepare for the test. Some dance around the caged, snarling quickdeath. The priest and several others seem to be discussing something.

You start to wonder if you can just sneak away and avoid the whole dreadful thing.

"Rise, Kyiki. It is time." The priest slowly places a red, purple, and white scarf around your neck, then removes your belt pouches.

The V-shaped lines form again, with the priest at the point. But this time there are many more Edestekai, some small, young ones, falling in behind. The whole village must want to watch you die!

You are led to an open area near the village, decorated with red, purple, and white ribbons on poles.

As you walk you wish desperately that the priest had not thought to take away your pouches. But even your Stunstick may not have been of much use against that creature.

At the far side of the clearing, the priest says, "Remain here."

The Edestekai circle the clearing, the young ones bouncing with excitement.

Then you see it. A wheeled cage is being pulled down the path from the village. Inside is the huge quickdeath. You see again the horrifying teeth, the razor-sharp claws, the waving tentacles. . . .

The wagon reaches level ground. An Edestekai runs out into the clearing, puts down an animal of some kind, and then returns to the wagon and unlatches the wagon's door.

In a flash, the quickdeath is out of the wagon and across the clearing. Its tentacles flash around the small animal and shove it into its great gaping mouth.

"Kyiki," the priest asks, "are you ready for the Test of Truthfulness?"

You want desperately to shout, "NO!" But you know you HAVE told the truth. If you must fight this horrible thing to be believed, you'll just have to fight.

"I am ready!" you say loudly and firmly.

"Young Kyiki, you have seen the jaws of justice and still you are ready to fight it. Now we know that you are telling the truth. We accept your word."

You breathe a long, deep sigh.

"Come," says the priest. "Let us go radio to your father."

THE END

"I don't see how we're going to get out of here," you say. "Let's let the guards know we're awake and see what happens."

"Hey! Hold it right there!" exclaims a human as you lean through the opening. "Thu-ju Kip wants to see you." After a few minutes, the evil-looking Thu-ju Kip enters.

"All right. Who are you?" the big Yazirian demands fiercely.

"I am Kyiki, a student," you say, trying to sound brave, "and this is Jac, my tutor. We were on a trip to view this planet, when our ship crashed. We'd like to go home. Perhaps we could radio a ship to get us."

"Oh, your family has so many spaceships that it can just call on one to casually stop by for you?" Thu-ju Kip says sarcastically.

"No, sir. But my father is the head of Universal Minerals, which has many ships. He'd send one for us, if we could radio."

"Universal Minerals, eh? Maybe that ship could bring a nice big pile of money."

"I'm sure he'd be happy to pay you for any inconvenience we've caused you."

"We'll just have a chat with your father about how much you're worth to him!"

It's scary being a piece of pirate treasure. But your father will soon know you are alive on Volturnus. And if you don't give the pirates any trouble, maybe you'll still be in one piece when you're ransomed.

THE END

"There are lots of pirates and only five crewmen. I know there are only two of us, but seven's better than five," you say.

"This is not the sort of learning experience I promised your father I would provide," Jac says sternly.

"Come on, Jac. We've GOT to help them."

"All right, Kyiki," Jac sighs.

You go back into the hut, where the crew is busily distributing the weapons.

"We're with you!" you say proudly.

"Never doubted it for a moment," says the Yazirian. "Grab a stunner."

You turn to look for the sonic stunners, but instead your eyes are caught by a box of grenades.

"Hey, look! Doze grenades. Lots of them."

"So?" grunts one of the strange Vrusk.

"There are lots more of them than there are of us. If we can knock out whole bunches of them at once, we'll even the odds."

"Good thinking, kid," the Yazirian says, then suggests a way to ambush the pirates.

You hide in the branches of a tree that hangs over the unloading area. As you wait nervously, a green flying creature lands on the branch beside you, chippering happily.

"Okay, Pongo," you say. "You can help."

At last you hear the telltale roar of the hovercars and truck. The truck draws up in the open area below you. You grab a grenade and wait until all the pirates are out of the truck. Okay . . . now!

-ROSLOF

You throw the grenade hard against the side of the truck. It explodes in a cloud of mist. Three pirates next to the point of impact fall to the ground instantly. Two others start to run, then they, too, fall.

As you toss the next grenade, Jac throws another from a different tree. Suddenly doze grenades are exploding all around the pirates. Several draw their weapons but can't find anyone to aim at, and they fire blindly into the trees.

Then the cargo ship's crew begins closing in, firing at the remaining pirates. Finally the Yazirian shouts, "Come on down. We've got to lock them up before they come to. Doze grenades don't last long."

It takes all of you to move the pirates into huts and lock them in. A few begin to stir, but they are quickly subdued.

You're all breathing heavily by the time the last pirate is locked up.

"What do we do now?" you ask the Yazirian breathlessly.

"Let's get back to the ship and see how the captain is. Then we'll call your father and tell him about you and the pirates."

As you head toward the cargo ship, you begin to think about the essay you'll write describing what you learned on Volturnus. For once, you won't mind writing "How I Spent My Vacation."

THE END

Most of all you want to get away from these weird characters. You'd rather face the wilds of an unknown planet than continue to be a captive.

You can't get out the main door. Every time you've been near it, you've been sent away. But the Boss could!

You don the belt and insert the disc. You know that the disc will work on its own but only for a few minutes. You need the powerpack in the belt to make the holographic image last long enough for you to get away.

Before you have time to change your mind, you open your door and move out into the corridor. There's no slinking for you this time.

When you turn the corner in the corridor, you see a Yazirian standing in a doorway. You hesitate a moment but then walk steadily on by. The Yazirian turns its head and looks at you with its black monkey eyes but allows you to pass. You struggle not to rush around the next corner. You try to walk casually . . .

Right into the arms of Gorlo, the Dralasite who originally kidnapped you!

"Boss!" Gorlo exclaims. "How did you get here?" Before you have a chance to answer, you feel the holobelt slipping loose from the impact of the collision with the Dralasite.

Grabbing the belt, you pull it back up around your waist. But it's too late. You have accidentally disconnected the powerpack from the disc. For just a moment, your true self was visible.

"The kid!" Gorlo exclaims. "So you took the disc. And you thought you were going to escape, huh? Well, you've got another think coming. No more wandering around for you, kid."

Gorlo takes the belt and disc from you and marches you through sections of Eorna you've never seen before. As you are led down the damp, dark corridors, you wonder how long you'll spend in a lonely cell before you are ransomed by your father.

THE END

"I think we'd be likely to find surveyors near a river, Ting," you say.

The land gets more interesting as you move around the base of the mountain. "There are craters, Ting, like those on many moons."

At first you see only a few craters. Then they get more and more frequent, until the surface is honeycombed with them.

You round a bend to see a mighty river cascading down the side of the mountain. The river swirls into frothing whirlpools in the basins of the craters and disappears.

"It's beautiful, Ting," you say in awe. And at Ting's insistence, you describe it to him in great detail, including the brown spongy-looking surface of the land.

"You say the river simply disappears? Let's go look!"

"Hey, Ting! I thought Dad programmed you to give me advice, not to lead me astray. We're supposed to be finding help."

"Well, decide, Kyiki."

1) "The foothills farther on are rocky and wooded. There might be people there to help." If this is your choice, turn to page 67.

2) "I'm really curious about the river, too, Ting. I want to see where it goes." Turn to page 143.

There's a chronocom on your wrist, with a short-range radio built in. Maybe help is somewhere nearby.

Ever so slowly, you reach your right hand to your left wrist and click on the chronocom's broadcast unit. Then you inch your left wrist toward your mouth.

You speak in as loud a whisper as you dare, hoping the Dralasite won't hear you over the roar of the hovercycle.

"Mayday! Mayday! This is Kyiki. I am being kidnapped. I repeat, I— Ouch!"

"Oh, no, you don't!" the Dralasite exclaims angrily. It yanks your left arm up behind your back. You twist your body, trying to escape the awful pain in your shoulder.

"Let me go!" you shout in anger, and, almost without thinking, you shove at the gray shapeless figure with your right arm.

The Dralasite loses its balance. The hovercycle leans way over and the cushion of air is broken. The machine crashes to the ground, partly on top of the Dralasite.

Jerking free from its grasp, you leap away from the hovercycle. You want to run, but your arm hurts unbearably.

"Blasted kid!" growls the Dralasite as it gets to its feet. "The pipes from the compressor are smashed. You'll pay for that!" it growls.

It pulls out a zapgun and points it at you. "Get marching, kid!" it demands.

You stand up and grab Ting from the pouch

on the hovercycle, determined not to lose your friend. "Which way, sir?" you ask.

It points impatiently toward the low hills. "Get moving! They're expecting us."

You don't know who "they" are, but you'd better not ask right now. You start to walk, the Dralasite following close behind.

You walk across an open sandy plain. The sun is intense, but a brisk wind keeps you cool.

Occasionally you see large flat dark shapes carried by the wind across the plain. One drifts near you, and you see that it's a giant leaf, perhaps three meters in diameter. It looks thick and tough.

You realize that you must do something. You've got to get away from this mad creature!

You appear to have three choices:

1) Run away. Turn to page 58.

2) Hop onto one of those large floating leaves and go wherever it goes. Turn to page 8.

3) Keep walking and play along with whatever happens. Otherwise, you might never learn what's behind the kidnapping. Turn to page 56.

"We've got to go now, while the door is open. If they close it when we're standing here, we really will be stuck!" you say.

"All right, Kyiki. But, remember, we have no idea who is on that ship." You run toward the ship. Jac follows slowly. A human and two powerful Yazirians are working in the open cargo bay.

"Hey!" you shout. They look up, startled.

"What are you doing on Volturnus?" asks the human.

Quickly you tell your story. "My dad will be worried about me," you add. "He's the head of Universal Minerals."

"Oh! That's who this cargo is for. There's a mineral survey party arriving."

"Good," says Jac. "I think the sooner we get this young person home, the better."

"Well, we were going to check out this equipment, but . . . you're right. The sooner we get going, the better."

As soon as the ship leaves the atmosphere of Volturnus, the captain radios Universal Minerals and asks urgently for your father.

"Yes, Captain? What's so important?"

"Kyiki and his tutor are here with me. Their spaceship crashed on Volturnus. I found them and am bringing them home."

"Nonsense! Kyiki just left here a little while ago. The ship won't even be near Volturnus for several hours. There must be some sort of mix-up. Maybe even an imposter."

Then you remember that you turned the

time machine to place you in a slightly earlier time. Your father doesn't know that the laboratory ship crashed. Maybe it hasn't even happened yet!

But you have an idea. If the ship hasn't crashed yet, maybe you can keep it from happening!

"Dad!" you shout into the radio. "It's really me, Kyiki. And Jac is with me."

"You certainly do sound like Kyiki. I just don't understand."

"Listen, Dad. I can explain what happened — I think. But you have to warn the lab ship that it's going to crash!"

"What nonsense! How can you possibly know that?" your father growls. "Captain? I don't know what this is all about, but bring your passengers back here. I just hope this isn't some kind of a trick. Keep an eye on them."

"Right, sir," the captain says, and he looks at you suspiciously as he signs off.

Sighing, you sit back, knowing the captain is not going to listen to you. But then you realize that if you could prevent the laboratory ship from crashing, you wouldn't be here now . . . and if you're not here now, you can't prevent the ship from crashing.

Your mind spinning, you grab hold of the one comforting thought—your father will straighten everything out when you get home.

THE END

"Dad said there aren't many big animals on Volturnus," you tell Ting.

"And what do you conclude from that?" asks the Compu-Pal.

"Ting! Stop sounding so much like Jac! One tutor is enough," you complain. "I CONCLUDE that there might be someone near that herd of animals who can help us."

Taking the food and water you find in the PSP and storing it in your ample pouches, you pick up Ting and head toward the dust cloud.

You stop only once, to mix the water with Nutrijuice powder and drink it down. Then you look back and realize that what you thought was a flat plain has actually been rising slightly as you walked. Ahead of you in the distance are mountains.

Please turn to page 39.

You're never allowed out of the room, which is pleasant but sparsely furnished. You notice there is no mirror. These thugs probably never use one, you decide.

You find plenty to do. Occasionally you try to question one of the guards, but you never get answers to your questions.

Finally, Gorlo, the Dralasite, comes to your cell. Instead of pulling up a chair, it just changes its shape into a ball. It rocks gently on its bottom as it talks.

"Well, Kyiki. There's been some delay. We haven't been able to reach your father. However, you have been behaving. Do you want to get out of this room?"

"And go home?" you ask excitedly.

"No, not home. Just out of this room. Dirk, the human, thinks you would behave. And there are plenty of us to keep an eye on you."

"I won't cause trouble. I'd like to get around more." To yourself, you add, "And maybe I can find a way to get out of here."

In the next few days, you wander freely around the elaborate complex. It is the most beautiful place you've ever seen. You learn that it is part of a huge city left by beings called the Eorna. A few Eorna still live on Volturnus, but most were killed by the Sathar, enemy of all civilized planets.

Everywhere you turn you find unexpected beauty—a sculpture, a tiny garden. You also find evidence that your captors have destroyed some of its beauty.

You also make other discoveries. You find rooms filled with weapons. The guards fight among themselves a great deal and often refer to their fear of the Boss. They don't seem to notice the beauty around them.

One day you are wandering through the corridors, wishing you could get some exercise outdoors. You follow an interesting silver pattern in the wall. When you near a corner in the corridor, you hear two guards talking.

"Have you ever met a Sathar?" one asks.

"Nope," the other says. "All our dealings with them are through the Boss."

"The Boss gives me the creeps! Are you sure there's only one of him? He seems to be everywhere at once. Sometimes I swear he's a hologram and all we're seeing is lots of images of him! Say, you don't suppose that's what's on that mystery holodisc he keeps locked up, do you?"

"Nah! I guess that's why he's the Boss—he always knows what's going on."

You hear footsteps move off down the corridor and the voices fade. But you've heard enough to set your mind spinning.

The Boss a hologram! What a wild idea!

You've seen your parents use holograms of sculptures around your home. They're like three-dimensional photographs suspended in space. You think you see the real piece of sculpture, but it's not really there.

You've heard that some people make holographic images of famous people to wear at parties. The image forms all around the person wearing it. Someone else sees only the holographic image, not the wearer. That's what Gorlo, the Dralasite, must have been wearing when it appeared as Jac.

Suddenly the voice of a Kurabanda interrupts your thinking.

"The kid's got to be around here somewhere. He can't wander far," you hear.

You hurry back to the main lounge, where you spend much of your time.

"There you are," says Gorlo. "Come on. The Boss wants you to talk to your father."

"Dad?" you question excitedly.

"Now, don't get excited," Gorlo says. "We've finally contacted him, and he needs a little persuading that you're really here with us before he gives us a little gift—a gift the Sathar won't ever need to hear about." It chuckles secretly. "So you're just going to chat a few minutes, saying just what we tell you."

You've never been to the radio room before. As you go, you wonder how you can make this chance work for you. What can you do to let your father know more than they want him to?

In the center of the radio room is a huge radio. You wait for Sparks, the Vrusk radio engineer, to tune the radio. Gorlo hands you a piece of paper.

"Read it just the way it is," Gorlo demands. "Don't try any tricks!"

"Okay," you agree. "I'll do as you say."

"Give me your radio key," Sparks says.

You clutch the crystal key hanging around your neck under your shirt. "How did you know I have one?"

"Come on, kid. We know everything there is to know about you and your dad. He gave you that key several years ago, when you started traveling. Now, hand it over!"

You pull out the chain and hand Sparks the key. The engineer inserts it into a slot.

Instantly, the hum of the radio changes to a clean silence. You hear some noises coming from far, far away.

"Kyiki?" The sound of your father's familiar voice fills the room. The engineer turns the volume down slightly.

You have only a moment to decide:

1) You can say what your captors want you to say, and no more, and be safe. If this is your choice, turn to page 22.

2) You can try to work some clues into your conversation with your father that will tell him where you are. If this is your choice, turn to page 87.

3) Or you can quickly try to tell your father where you are and hope for the best. If this is your choice, turn to page 26.

"Surveyors have got to be fascinated by a disappearing river. I'm sure we'll find help there."

"You reason as you want, Kyiki," says Ting.

"Huh? What do you mean?"

"Think about it," answers Ting.

You walk toward the river, feeling spray in your face as you near the whirlpools. Then the roar quietens as the river enters the brown spongy mass.

Seeing some of the strange brown stuff beneath your feet, you bend down and touch it. It has a smooth, tough texture.

"It's like something I've seen before," you say thoughtfully. "Oh, yes. It's like the fungus that grows on trees at home, but much, much larger—large enough for a whole huge river to disappear into."

"Fascinating!" says Ting. "I sometimes regret the sight limitations placed on me by the manufacturing facility. I'd like to see it."

You want to see the place where the river disappears, so you step onto the funguslike stuff. It sinks slightly beneath your feet.

"It's kind of soft but tough at the same time—like a firm mattress."

"Don't be in any great hurry, Kyiki."

You keep walking, taking care where you step. Suddenly you sniff. The air doesn't feel quite right. It doesn't really smell of anything — it just seems strange. But it's nice. You smile. It makes you feel good.

You walk on, feeling happy. You sink a bit as you walk, but that doesn't matter. You whistle a tune, wishing a songbird would answer. Well, that doesn't matter either.

"Tell me what's happening, Kyiki."

With each step you take, you sink deeper and deeper into the fungus. Somehow, that strikes you as funny, and you bubble with laughter.

"Kyiki! Talk to me!" demands Ting. But you just laugh and toss the computer in the air, then step forward to catch it.

Suddenly you can't pull your foot out. You are mired in the quickfungus, but you don't care. The gas it gives off is like laughing gas. The fact that you're stuck, maybe forever, strikes you as very funny.

"Kyiki! Tell me what's happening! That must be the funniest joke in the whole world!"

Swaying with laughter, your feet held firmly by the fungus, you don't even notice that you're in trouble. What a fun way to reach . . .

THE END

Moving through the green woods, you see small structures set in a clearing.

"Maybe we can get help here," you say.

You look at the buildings more closely. You see no motion of any kind.

SNAP!

That wasn't you! Heart pounding, you step quickly back behind a tree.

"Easy, Kyiki," you hear Jac say under his breath as he crouches low in the grass.

Holding your breath, you move your head just enough to see around the tree trunk. There, just inches below your eyes, are the frightened brown eyes of a creature. You look it up and down—a green furry animal with skin-covered wings and a big mouth like a frog's. You smile and the creature's eyes relax and turn friendly.

The creature climbs up the tree, spreads its wings, and flies to your shoulder.

You pet, tickle, then wrestle with the creature. Within minutes, it is your friend.

"Pongo! I'll call you Pongo," you say.

Pongo takes you by the hand and leads you, with Jac following, into the clearing. The place seems curiously deserted.

The village consists of quickly built, uncomfortable-looking shacks.

"Do you think anyone lives here?" you ask, puzzled.

"Hard to tell," answers Jac. "There's certainly no one here now." He moves to the door of a hut slightly larger than the others.

"Curious," he mutters. "This door is locked. Why would that be?" he asks himself.

Leaving Jac to his pondering, you begin to explore, Pongo at your heels. Suddenly it flies up into a tree and begins to drop its fruit on your head.

"Stop that, Pongo! Come down here!"

The creature glides from the tree, lands at your heels, and starts going through your belt pouch. It grabs something, dashes up a tree, and then throws the object far away.

"Pongo! That's my Stunstick! I just got it for my birthday. Blast you, Pongo!"

You run after the Stunstick and finally find it in the grass. You pick up the treasured gift and return it to your pouch. When you look up, you notice a large circular platform made of stone. In the middle stands a large, complicated-looking crystalline structure.

You step up on the platform to inspect the structure. It's about two meters high on its pedestal, with long white crystals jutting out at odd angles all around it.

You touch some of the long crystals in awe. Nothing moves.

Then you notice a round knob between crystals at the center of the structure. You reach in past the crystals and grasp it. It turns slightly, and suddenly there is a great, blinding flash.

You jerk your hand back from the crystal and the light dies.

"What have I done?" you whisper in horror and turn to look for your tutor. But he's no longer by the locked hut. In fact, there's nothing there! The shacks are gone. Jac is gone. And something seems wrong with the trees. They are smaller and younger than they were a few minutes ago!

What happened? You pinch yourself to see if you're dreaming. But you're awake.

Maybe the crystal structure has something to do with it. You did turn the knob slightly. Maybe you should turn it back. You hesitate. What if something drastic happens? But what else can you do?

Reaching into the crystal structure again, you grasp the knob. "Here goes nothing!" you think and, eyes closed, turn it slightly.

Slowly you turn your head and open one eye to peek behind you.

It's okay! You breathe a deep sigh of relief. There is Jac, standing where he was before, near one of the shacks. And there is Pongo, swinging by one foot from a branch.

Walking over to Jac, you say, "Uh, Jac, I've got to tell you something." You hesitate, not sure he'll believe your story.

But then you notice Jac's peculiar expression. "What's the matter?" you ask.

"I . . . I don't know. There was a great light, and then I seemed to fade away just for a moment," Jac confesses hesitantly.

"You don't know how glad I am to hear that!"

"Glad? Why are you glad?" Jac is puzzled.

"Well, I was wondering how to tell you what

just happened to me, but I guess it happened to you, too." And you explain, somewhat confusedly, what happened.

"Hmmmm," murmurs Jac, thinking. "Maybe it's some sort of time device. You moved the knob only slightly, so time turned back only slightly. Younger trees, no camp . . ." Then the Vrusk gets excited.

"What a wonderful find! Why, we could have living Volturnian history lessons!"

You and Jac go back to the stone circle to examine the crystalline structure. The Vrusk pokes and prods but avoids touching the knob in the center.

"Well, young one. Do you want to see Volturnian history firsthand?" he asks, rather like a child with a new toy, you think.

1) If you choose to try the time machine again, turn to page 74.

2) If you decide to stay in your own time so that you won't miss being rescued, turn to page 31.

"Let's try to get the guard out of the room. Then we can radio a message to my dad," you say.

"What is your plan?" Arnla asks.

"Well . . . we passed a side room just a little way back down the corridor. Maybe we can trick the guard into going in there while I use the radio."

You backtrack down the corridor to a room where you glimpsed a light as you passed earlier. The light you saw, you now discover, is the glow of molten lava.

A hot blast hits you as you enter the room. The floor of the cave is a pool of bubbling, glowing red lava. A ledge, wide on one side and narrow on the other, circles the pool.

Ignoring the loud blub-blub of the bubbling lava, you tell Arnla the rest of your plan. Then you return to the door.

"Help! . . . Help!" you shout.

You hear a chair screech again and you hide behind the doorway.

"What's that? . . . Who's there?" the Kurabanda guard calls as it comes through the door.

You stay perfectly still, hidden in the shadows, as the guard looks around, pistol at the ready. It sees Arnla across the lava pool on the wide ledge.

"An Ul-Mor!" it exclaims. "What're you doing here?" It starts toward Arnla.

Arnla looks young and frightened. She whimpers helplessly, looking quite harmless.

"Hey! How'd you get down here, anyway?" The Kurabanda bends down to grab Arnla. She quickly scurries past it.

The guard follows her and says, "It's all right. You don't have to be afraid."

You edge toward the door, but you want to be absolutely certain Arnla can keep the guard occupied.

The guard reaches her. Arnla wraps her tentacles around its legs. It struggles and drops the pistol. With a loud hiss, the pistol disappears in the molten lava.

"Hey! I won't hurt you. Let go!" the Kurabanda pleads.

Arnla releases the guard. It backs away, thinks a minute, and then holds out its hand again.

"It's all right, little Ul-Mor. I'm not going to hurt you. I want to help you."

But once more Arnla wraps her arms around its legs, then releases it again.

"All right. I guess I'll have to go get help." The guard turns to walk the other way around the pool, but it is forced to stop when the narrow edge dwindles to a few centimeters.

It's safe to go now. Arnla will keep the guard trapped on the other side of the pool. It doesn't know you're there, so it probably won't start shouting.

You step out into the corridor and see two other guards walking away from you. They must have come out of the radio room. You're glad you decided not to attack the guard!

You stop and peer into the radio room. Fortunately, there's no one in sight.

A large radio hangs from the ceiling. What luck! It's just like your father's.

You pull your personal radio crystal out from under your shirt. It fits any radio but works for your voice and no other. It automatically broadcasts only on the frequency of your home radio.

You inspect the radio hurriedly, then pull out its crystal and insert your own.

You lean forward and whisper, "Hello. This is Kyiki. Hello, Dad?"

Nothing happens. Holding your breath, you adjust the crystal slightly. Immediately you can tell that you have a live radio.

"Hello, Dad. This is Kyiki," you repeat. "I'm in trouble and need your help."

You pause, then your father's voice answers, "What can I do, Kyiki?"

You quickly explain. When you tell him about the surveyors' deal with the Sathar, you hear a brief sputter.

Your father breaks in. "There's a Universal Minerals starliner approaching Volturnus now. I'll have a shuttle sent down to pick you up. Did you set the automatic beacon on your PSP?"

"Yes, but the antenna's broken."

"They'll be able to pick up the signal when they get close. Meet them near the PSP. I'll send others to deal with those traitors. So long, Kyiki. See you soon. Over and out."

What a relief! You'll soon be on your way home, if you can get back to your PSP.

Yanking your crystal from the radio, you head back to the lava pool.

The Kurabanda guard is still caught in Arnla's tentacles. Each time it struggles, she tips it toward the lava.

"It's okay to release it now, Arnla," you say.

To the guard, you say, "Walk back as far as you can on the narrow ledge. She'll leave you alone as long as you don't try to get past her."

Arnla lets go and the guard backs off, muttering crossly.

You sit on the floor by Arnla. She connects her ninth tentacle and you tell her about your conversation with your father.

"Wonderful, Kyiki. I'm glad you'll be going home. But how will we escape without the guard alerting everyone?"

"Uh-oh! I haven't thought about that! The minute we leave, it'll warn the others." You look around but see nothing that could be used to tie up the Kurabanda.

But your eye does catch something else. Between you and the guard, one narrow part of the ledge is badly undercut. Only a thin shelf of rock remains. And you're sure you see a thin crack, several meters long, running through the rock shelf. You grow excited as an idea begins to form.

Arnla catches your excitement and follows your gaze. Her face lights as she sees what you have in mind.

"We could break off the ledge and the guard wouldn't be able to get past the break. And its shouts wouldn't be heard over the bubbling lava," she says excitedly.

In the corridor, you find a heavy pole—a long metal rod with a flag on the top, used in surveying.

You hurry back to the lava room. You've got to act fast before the guard realizes what you're up to.

You dig the rod down into the crack and lean on it hard.

Nothing happens, and the guard starts toward you. You try again in another place, and then again.

"Hey! What are you doing?" shouts the Kurabanda, moving more quickly now.

Ignoring it, you plant your feet firmly and try once again.

CRA-A-A-A-ACK! The ledge breaks loose and plunges into the lava below.

You sigh as you see that the missing section is at least five meters long. The guard won't be able to leap over that.

"Come on, Arnla. Let's hurry. The other guards may return any time."

As you leave, you see the monkeylike guard jumping up and down at the edge of the lava pool, its shouts of rage lost in the loud, echoing blub-blub of the lava.

As you and Arnla hurry back, you think of getting home. You'll miss Arnla. She's been a true friend on this strange, unfriendly planet.

Maybe you can visit when your father is working at the new mining sites.

There's daylight up ahead. Now that you know you can get home, you feel an urge to stay and explore this strange planet further. But on the frontiers of the stars, there will always be new worlds to explore.

THE END